Dude's Gotta
Mountain Bike

Muddy Frank

Dude's Gotta Mountain Bike
French Marmot Dude Series
ISBN: 978-2-9562556-9-7
Text by Muddy Frank
Cover Illustration by Uniqueupe

Author note: Dude, this book has British spelling.

369FAD7410574CCC458009758186ACEF05FBFFDBFEDD5DE82F0E2A482BEEF174

"There is more treasure in books
than in all the pirate's loot
on Treasure Island."

— Walt Disney

Mishka

Magali

Henri Le Hare

F-F-Foxy

Little Foxy

Puppy Bébé

Chamois Luc

Medical Ed The Eagle

Some mountain bike tricks:

Frontflip	Do a forward somersault on a bike.
Backflip	Do a backward somersault on a bike.
Barspin	Spinning the handlebars around in a complete circle.
360	A 360° rotation in the air, to one side.
Bunny Hop	A jump in the air, first the with the front wheel, then the back.
Tailwhip / Hop Whip	Kick the back end of the bike in a full rotation around the handlebars.
Truck Driver	A 360 with a barspin.
Can Can	The person takes one foot off the pedal and kicks the leg over the top tube.
Kicker	It's a ramp.

CONTENTS

Chapter 1
Hop And Bop

Heavy golden bells hung around the cows' necks, clanging each time they trotted up the mountain. The faster the cows trotted, the faster the bells rang. *Clang! Clang! Clang!*

Magali couldn't believe it. 'No! No! No! They're out of time. Their bells are ringing at different times.' She placed her paws over her tiny marmot ears. She shouted to the cows, 'I'm so embarrassed for you!' She watched them from her hiding place, with her best mate, Mishka.

The cows climbed higher, passing The Cheese Shack. It's a wooden cabin where Big People wear white aprons, and on their hair, they wear little mosquito nets. Inside, there are huge, steel pots filled with milky liquid. The Big People use long sticks to turn the milky liquid around and around, until one day they pull out an enormous lump of fresh cheese.

On the mountain, a Big Person, wearing long black boots and a black cap, followed the cows. He called to them. 'Eeeeeeeeeh-up, up, up!' Each time he yelled, the cows moved faster. They trotted, and one of them lifted her tail and did a sloppy poop.

Mishka's rabbit eyes nearly exploded. He pointed. 'She didn't even stop! She trotted and pooped at the same time!'

Poop slid down the cow's leg.

'Eeeeeeeeeeyuuuew!' Magali squished up her nose.

'Eeeeeeeeeh-up, up, up!' The Big Person called.

The marmot and rabbit put their paws around their mouths, and shouted, 'Eeeeeeeeeh-up, up, up!'

A cow with great big pointy horns turned and stared. Magali and Mishka gasped, then disappeared behind their rock. After a minute, they stuck their heads out again.

'Yoo-hoo! Here we are!' called Mishka.

A large shepherd dog came running. *Grrrrrrrrrrrrrrrrrrrrrrrr. Ruff! Ruff!*

'Run!' shouted Magali.

The marmot and rabbit raced like wildfire across the mountain. They sped up and down mounds, over pebbles, dirt tracks, grassy patches, and blue, yellow, and white flowers. They raced till they reached the clearing outside Mishka's home. They hunched over, gasping for breath and wiping sweat from their brows.

'Good!' said Mishka's mother in her Dutch accent when she saw them arrive. 'You can help me clean the burrow. Your cousins are arriving tomorrow, Mishka.' She wore her long ears tied up in a knot on top of her head.

The young rabbit and marmot followed Mishka's mother into the underground burrow.

Inside, the mother rabbit nodded to a wooden broom in the corner. 'First, you sweep the kitchen, then you sweep the bedroom. We want your cousins to get a good impression. Okay?'

Mishka nodded.

'Good. When you finish that, you can throw out the old hay and make fresh new hay beds. We want your cousins to sleep well. Okay?'

Mishka nodded.

'Good. When you finish that, you wipe down the table and arrange the wooden bowls in their place.

Then you stack the apricots. We want your cousins to be properly fed. Okay?'

Mishka nodded.

When Mishka's mama hopped outside, Mishka looked at Magali and said, 'Sorry. We came back at the wrong time.'

'That's okay,' said the fat marmot, picking up the broom.

'Hop and Hop, and Bop and Bop!' Mishka's little brothers and sisters hopped into the burrow, one after the other, singing at the top of their voices. *'Hop and Hop, and Bop and Bop! Hop and Hop, and Bop and Bop!'*

Magali tried to count the tiny rabbits as they hopped in their conga line. 'One, two, three, four, five, six, seven, eight, nine, ten, eleven, oh my goodness, how many, twelve, thirteen, seriously how many little brothers and sisters, fourteen, fift... '

'Out!' yelled Mishka.

The tiny rabbits stopped. They looked at their brother.

Mishka pointed to the burrow door. Sunshine poured in through the hole. 'Out!' repeated Mishka. 'We have to clean up, so you can't be here.'

The little rabbits ignored their brother and

continued singing and dancing. *'Hop and Hop and Bop and Bop!'*

'Ouuuuuuuuuttt!' yelled Mishka.

'Alright. No need to shout,' said a baby rabbit, slumping his shoulders. He led the others to the front door. One by one, they hopped out of the hole, up onto the mountain and into the fresh air.

Mishka turned to Magali. 'Let's do this quickly so we can go back outside and play.'

'Yes!' Magali started sweeping. She liked visiting Mishka's burrow because it was so different to her burrow. Her burrow smelt like lovely tree bark. Mishka's burrow smelt like fresh hay. Her kitchen was round. Mishka's kitchen was rectangular. It had a long wooden table for all the rabbits to fit around at breakfast, lunch, and dinner.

'Oh my goodness!' Mishka's mother came racing into the burrow. Her ears had fallen out of their knot. 'They're here!'

'Who?' asked Mishka.

'Your cousins!'

'What?'

'They're here! I can see them coming up the mountain!' Mishka's mother looked at the dirt floor and all the unwashed wooden bowls on the table. 'We're not ready! They're going to think we're pigs! Aaaaaaaaaaaaaaaaaaaaagh!'

'Mama, relax. They're family.'

'No, Mishka. Your Aunty Anita is neat-freak! What are we going to do?' She started hopping in circles. Her bunny tail boinged up and down.

Magali started collecting all the bowls from the wooden table and stacking them in the cupboard.

'They're not washed!' Mishka's mother screamed, pulling Magali back.

Mishka ran to his mother and shook her shoulders. 'Mama! Stop! It's going to be alright.'

Mishka's mother looked at her son. 'I haven't seen my sister since we left Holland. My floor isn't swept, my dishes aren't done and my beds aren't changed. And you're telling me it's going to be alright?! IT'S NOT ALRIGHT, MISHKA!' yelled his mother. Red veins appeared in her left blue eye.

'*Hop and Hop and Bop and Bop!*' Baby rabbits came dancing inside. 'They're nearly here!'

Mishka's mother grabbed Magali. 'Honey, you've got to go.' She pushed the plump marmot towards the front door.

'What?' Mishka said. 'Why?'

Mishka's mother pushed Magali through the entrance hole. 'Because.'

Mishka ran over and shouted up through the hole. 'Sorry, Magali! It's a madhouse! See you tomorrow!'

The very next day, Magali waited by the grassy mound. A bee flew up from the pink flowers and buzzed in front of her nose. She caught it, squished it, and swallowed it.

Mishka came up the mountain with two rabbits hopping behind him. 'Magali, these are my cousins,' said the rabbit when they got to her.

'Hello.' Magali smiled and moved forward to give a kiss hello on each cheek, cause that's how dudes say hello in France. *Mmmwua. Mmmwua.*

The rabbit with short, dark, spiky fur on his head introduced himself. 'Dangerous Dave. Dangerous for short.'

'Andy,' said the other rabbit with curly fur on his head.

They spoke in heavy Dutch accents.

'So, this is where you live, yeah?' Andy looked around at the wide open space. 'You going to give us the tour, or what?'

Mishka pushed his glasses high up on his nose. His pompon tail wiggled. 'Yes! First stop, the lake!'

'Yes, it's really pretty. You can see your reflection in the water!' said Magali.

'Sounds pretty mild. What sports do you do?'

'Uhm, we can go running over the mountain,' said Mishka.

'Picking flowers,' said Magali.

'We can play hide and seek,' added Mishka

Magali said, 'We can play tag.'

'We can visit The Cheese Farm!' Mishka's eyes lit up.

Magali frowned. 'You mean The Cheese Shack?'

'No. The Cheese Farm. It's on the other side of the forest, that way.' Mishka pointed.

'But what real sports can you do?' asked Dangerous.

Mishka looked at Magali. Magali looked back at Mishka.

'Where's the mountain biking?' asked Andy.

'Yeah!' Dangerous hopped up and down. The spiky fur on his head blew in the wind.

'I don't know,' said Mishka.

'What do you mean, you don't know?' said Andy.

'I don't know.'

Andy pointed up to the sky. Above them, Big People were sitting on the chairlift and moving up the mountain. Their bikes were attached to the backs of the chairlift. 'You sure you don't know?'

Mishka shrugged. He had seen the Big People and their bikes, but he didn't know what they did with them.

Magali shrugged too and shook her little head. Marmots' heads were flat-shaped and looked far too small for their fat, furry bodies.

'Man, you live in paradise with those Big People mountain biking, and you've never gone to watch them?'

Mishka squinted up at the top of the mountain, far away. He shook his head.

Andy looked at the fat marmot. 'And you?'

'I'm not allowed up that far on my own.'

'Good!' said Dangerous, slapping her shoulder. 'You're with us. Come on!' He waved for Magali and Mishka to follow. 'Let's follow the chairlift!'

Magali shook her head. 'I'm not allowed up that

high.'

Andy slapped her so hard on the back that she nearly fell over. 'Of course you are,' he said. 'You're with us.'

'I don't think it's a good idea.' The marmot rubbed the bald patch on her bottom. It was the size of two cherries.

Andy looked at Mishka. 'Man, we've never been to France before. Come on! Let's do this!'

The Dutch cousins started hopping up the mountain.

Mishka looked at Magali, blinking his blue eyes. 'It could be really fun. We're just going to go and see.'

Magali looked at the moving chairs in the sky.

Mishka saw her looking. He said, 'Maybe we'll find out how they move!'

Magali's almond-shaped eyes lit up. 'Do you think so?'

'Maybe.'

Magali nodded. 'Okay.'

They giggled as they followed Mishka's cousins up the grassy mountain, directly under the line of the chairlift.

'Keep an eye out for eagles,' said Mishka, hopping over a little mountain stream.

'Yeah, and foxes,' said Magali, stepping over wet rocks.

'We don't want to get eaten.'

The marmot shot Mishka a nervous smile. 'We're not going to get eaten. Right?'

Chapter 2
The Nose

A fat drop of sweat fell from Magali's forehead. 'Wow, it's hard work running straight uphill!'

Mishka sped alongside Magali. He looked up to the Big People in the chairs. 'Lucky them. They just have to sit.' Mishka huffed and puffed. 'We have to run up and down valleys.'

Magali nodded. 'And some really super steep parts.'

The higher they climbed, the fewer flowers they saw, the rockier the ground became, and the colder it got. They still sweated though as they scrambled up. Finally, they reached the top.

The happy foursome wiped sweat from their brows, took huge breaths in and high-fived each other. 'We did it!'

Magali stood on her tiptoes, looking around the immense space. She smiled as she recognised the shape of a blue ski run. 'Look! That's the Happy Days Piste!'

Mishka gave her a smile. 'Yes.'

The marmot pointed again. 'Wow! Look! Way down there. The lake! You can't see that in the winter.'

Magali covered her eyes from the sun. She squinted as she looked past the forest and towards the bottom of the valley.

Mishka said, 'You can't see everything. We're too high.'

Magali nodded. She looked up and across at the mountains way over on the other side of the valley. Even though it was summertime, snow covered the tops of the mountains, like vanilla ice-cream dripping down. 'It's so cool.'

'Look! It's Lazy Bones and Dopey Eyes!' Mishka pointed to the herd of cows from the other day. 'They've climbed up much higher.'

It was Andy's turn to point. 'Look!' Big People were getting off the Sugar Chairlift with their bikes. 'They're riding over to the right. We've got to follow them.' He looked up to the blue sky. 'But first, we need an escape plan in case we see an eagle. Or a fox. What are we going to do?'

'Run,' said Dangerous.

'Run,' said Mishka.

'Run,' said Magali.

Andy nodded. 'Okay, sounds like a plan. Let's go.'

Keeping as low to the ground as possible, the little animals crept along the mountain till they saw curvy tracks dug into the ground. The tracks looked like gigantic dirt snakes sliding down the mountain. Big People in helmets, gloves, and kneepads were riding down the curvy snake tracks, bouncing on dips and turns, following each other and cheering.

'Wow!' Magali's eyes opened so wide that they went from almond shape to plum shape.

'Ooooooh, that looks mad!' whispered Dangerous, his eyes lighting up.

'Look at that dude. He just flew over a bump!' whispered Andy, watching a Big Person fly over a kicker.

'Look at them riding down, one after the other. Look! Red helmet, yellow helmet, blue, green.'

'That one's going too fast, look he's going to...'

'Oooooh!' The three rabbits and the marmot gasped as they watched the Big Person in the purple helmet crash onto the rocky ground. Dirt sprayed up around him.

Big People riding down after him called as they rode past. 'Alright?'

The purple-helmet Big Person waved. 'I'm okay.' He dusted dirt off his pants and lifted up his bike.

Crouching in her hiding spot, Magali's eyes grew plum-shaped again as she watched the riders peddle hard, sit low on their bikes, hold on tightly to their handlebars, and ride over kickers. They flew into the air! Magali gasped. 'Wow!' She watched them land back on their back wheels and continue down the snakey track. 'Looks fun,' she whispered.

'Don't tell me you've never done it,' whispered Andy.

Mishka and Magali looked at Andy.

Dangerous said, 'No way! You live here in this paradise, and you've never been mountain biking?'

Mishka said, 'We don't come this high up the mountain usually.'

'Man, you need to try it. For sure, there are others that are doing it.'

'Rabbits?'

'Everyone,' said Dangerous. 'In Holland, all the guys go riding.'

'Right,' said Mishka. 'Well, I've never seen another animal riding a bike.'

'That's because you haven't been looking,' said Andy. 'I bet you three apricots that there are loads of dudes here that do it. At night, when the Big People aren't around.'

Dangerous Dave's eyes lit up. 'Let's come back tonight.'

Mishka's pompom tail wiggled. 'Yes!' He turned to the little marmot. 'Magali, do you... '

'I can't. Remember?'

'Oh, that's right,' said Mishka.

'Look!' Andy pointed, crouching lower. 'Get down!'

'What?' Dangerous looked across to the other side of the bike trail.

'What is it?' asked Mishka.

The fur on Magali's back spiked up. She looked across and saw what Andy and Dangerous saw.

On the other side of the bike trail, pointy fox ears poked out from behind a grassy mound. The foxes had been watching the Big People until they'd spotted the little animals on the other side. Now, their hungry fox eyes were staring straight at the rabbits and the fat, juicy marmot.

'Everyone stay calm,' whispered Andy.

Dangerous screamed, 'Ruuuuuun!

'Ruuuun!' shouted Mishka.

'Ruuuun!' screamed Magali.

The foxes leaped out from the mound and leaped over the bike trail.

'Eeeeeeeeeeeeeeeeeeeeeeeeeeeeeee!' squealed Magali, speeding down the mountain.

Mishka was right behind her. 'Faster! Hurry!'

Magali's little paws raced over the rocky ground. Her terrified eyes searched everywhere for a hiding space. She could hear the foxes behind them, panting and growling.

Grrrrrrrrrrrrrrrrrrrrrrrrrrrrrr.

Her Papa had told her, "Foxes will chase you, catch you, and make marmot stew out of you. They like young marmots. Your meat is soft and juicy."

'Here! Quick!' Magali raced towards a hole in the ground. She squashed her little body through the hole.

Mishka hopped behind and dived in head-first. Magali pulled. 'Sorry!' she said as she pulled his head. *Pop!* Suddenly, Mishka's whole body squeezed through.

Very small animals must have made the burrow because there was only just enough room for Magali and Mishka to sit in.

Suddenly, the little stream of sunlight from outside disappeared and the burrow became dark.

'Ah!' Magali gasped, looking up at the entrance hole.

Snnnnifff, snnnnniff, snnnnnifff. A black nose poked through the hole.

Magali and Mishka pressed back against the burrow wall as much as they could, but the fox's nose was close, close enough for them to touch it if they'd wanted to.

The fox's wet nose sniffed up and down, moving faster when he smelt how close the marmot and the rabbit were.

'No!' Mishka cried, his frightened blue eyes fixated on the fox nose.

Suddenly, the nose disappeared from the hole and scratching noises started.

'He's going to get us. He's digging,' whispered

Magali, looking around, trying to see how they could get out. 'We're trapped! He's going to get us!'

Mishka closed his eyes and started praying. 'Grandpa Klaas, if you can hear me, please help us. We really need your help. Make the fox go away.' Mishka did a little pee.

The fox's nose came back, pushing harder through the dirt hole. *Snnnnifff, snnnnniff, snnnnnifff.*

Tears rolled down Magali's cheeks as she pressed her back hard against the burrow wall. The nose got closer. She stretched out her super-sharp claws, getting ready to attack. She took a deep breath. Then, the fox's nose disappeared and sunlight streamed back in.

Magali and Mishka looked to the hole and the sunlight. They sat still, their ears standing up. They listened. Nothing.

'Is it a trap?' whispered Mishka.

'Maybe.'

The two friends sat, not daring to move in case the fox was waiting for them to stick their heads out.

They waited in the tiny burrow for a very long time. They waited and waited and waited.

Eventually, Magali took a deep breath. 'We have to

be brave. We have to look outside.'

'I don't want to,' whimpered Mishka.

'I know.'

'Can't we just stay here?'

'No,' whispered Magali. 'Whoever lives here will be coming back, so we need to get out.'

Mishka nodded. He took a big gulp of air, squared his shoulders and said, 'You're right. I'll go first.'

Magali watched as Mishka crept to the hole entrance. He looked back to Magali, bit his bottom lip, then ever so slowly poked his paw out of the hole. Fresh air blew on his paw. He pulled his paw back in and took a breath. He said one more little prayer to his Grandpa Klaas before sticking his head out.

'It's okay,' he whispered back to Magali. 'Give me a push.'

Magali pushed Mishka's bottom and he wriggled out of the hole. Next, Magali scrambled through the hole and jumped out. Her black eyes darted left and right, searching for danger.

'No foxes,' said Magali. 'Wonder why he left so quickly?'

Mishka looked up to the sky and did a little pee.

'That's why! Quick, get back in.' He pushed Magali back into the hole. Then he followed her, head-first. 'Pull!' he said to Magali.

She grabbed hold of his head and pulled him back in.

They lay inside on the dirt floor, huffing and puffing.

'Eagles,' said Mishka. 'And they know we're here now.'

'We're never going home,' said Magali.

Mishka suddenly remembered Andy and Dangerous. He took a big gulp. 'Where are my cousins?'

Chapter 3
Moving Chairlift

The next day, Magali met Mishka next to the mound with the pink flowers. 'Your cousins?' she asked.

The rabbit shook his head, looking at Magali with sad blue eyes.

'Oh no!'

'I know,' said Mishka, scratching his ear. 'I lied and told my mother and Aunty that they went over to Courchevel to visit old friends. I don't know if they believed me, but if I don't come back with them today, I'm in big trouble.'

'Do you think they're alright?' Magali looked up to the sky for eagles.

Mishka's eyes filled with water. His bottom lip

trembled.

Magali put her paw on her best mate's shoulder. 'Be positive. They are probably lost. They don't know the mountain.'

Mishka nodded, wiping a tear from under his glasses.

Magali said, 'Let's go back up the mountain where we were yesterday, and start from there. We'll find them.'

'Are you sure?' asked Misha.

'We have to.'

'And the eagles and the foxes?'

Magali smiled. 'We'll run faster!'

The marmot and rabbit looked up to the chairlift in the sky and started running over rocks and grass, following the Big People and their bikes up the mountain.

When they reached the top of the Sugar Chairlift, they crouched behind the same rock as yesterday. They watched Big People get off the chairlift and start riding the snakey dirt tracks.

Mishka looked over to see if he could see any foxes in the greenery, but he couldn't see anything. He looked up to the sky. Clear. He and Magali had had to wait a long time in that little burrow yesterday before they crept out again. Magali had made it home to her burrow just in time for dinner. Any later and she would have been in huge trouble. Her parents give her set times to be outside. Ever since the snowboarding adventure, they've become strict.

'This is where we were yesterday when the foxes came after us,' whispered Mishka, looking around. He pointed down the mountain. 'We ran that way.' He looked back up the mountain to the very top. 'Maybe Andy and Dangerous ran that way? Come on!'

Magali followed Mishka over the rocky mountain. She shivered. Even though the sun was shining, it was cold this high up the mountain. She nodded to the forest in the distance. 'If an eagle or fox comes, look, we run directly to the forest, okay?'

'Okay. But they're still going to get us.' Mishka looked around, scratching his head. 'Where could they have gone?'

They scrambled up as quickly as they could, all the time keeping an eye out for foxes and eagles. When they got to the very top, they looked over the other side and sighed.

'It's just another valley and mountain!' said Mishka, his shoulders dropping. He put his paws to his mouth and shouted, 'Andy! Dangerous! Where are youuuuuuuuu?'

Magali tugged Mishka's arm. 'Don't shout, Mishka. You let the eagles know we're here.'

'Sorry,' Mishka whispered. 'I'm worried.'

'I know.' Magali patted his shoulder.

They looked around them. All they could see were mountains, rock, and snow. All they could hear were Big People's voices shouting as they rode down the snakey trail.

Magali said, 'Let's go back to the chairlift, and instead of going right, we'll go left.'

They hurried back to their rock and looked over to the left.

'It doesn't make sense,' said Mishka. 'Why would they run straight in the direction where the foxes were coming from?' Mishka looked around the enormous mountain and a tear rolled down his face. 'How are we ever going to find them? It's too big.' He slumped his shoulders and dropped on to his knees.

Magali looked at the chairlift station. Big People were getting off with their bikes. She said, 'I have an idea!'

Five minutes later, the little duo hid next to the

Sugar Chairlift. Chairs arrived, swinging in the air as they got closer to the station. Magali and Mishka watched the Big People wriggle in their seats, getting ready to get off. The chairlift slowed down at the station whilst everyone got off with their bikes. Then, the chairs turned around and went back down the mountain, empty.

'What's your plan?' whispered Mishka.

'We take the chairlift down.' Magali eyed the empty chairs travelling back down.

'What?!'

'We take the chairs down.'

'Why?'

'We'll be able to see a whole lot more from up in the air, Mishka! We will be able to look left and right. It will save us so much time, don't you think?'

Mishka looked happy for the first time that day. He kissed Magali's cheek. 'Yes! You're a genius!'

Magali giggled. She looked to the chairlift. Crouching low, she whispered, 'We just have to time it properly so that we jump on the chair at the last minute, when it's going back down. And don't make any noise. And stay low. Hopefully, the Big People won't see us because they'll be too busy with their bikes.'

Mishka's blue eyes shone. He high-fived Magali. 'Let's do this.'

They crouched low in their hiding place and waited for the next chairlift to arrive into the station, and swing around.

'As soon as they get off this one, we'll go. On the count of three. Okay?'

Mishka nodded.

Magali focussed. She saw the empty chair turning around, nearly ready to leave the top of the mountain. 'One, two, three. Go!' She raced over the rocky ground and jumped onto the black leather chair. She lay as low and as still as she could. Mishka raced right behind her. He jumped, missed, and landed on the rocky ground just below. He started sliding down the mountain.

Magali's eyes nearly popped out of her head when she saw Mishka on the ground. She turned her head, looking back. 'Get the next one! Quickly! Jump up! Hurry, Mishka!'

Mishka's paws dug into the ground to stop him sliding and he scrambled up the mountain and jumped on the next chair. He lay low. His body trembled all over. The chair took him away from the chairlift station, into the air.

Magali sat frozen in the chair in front. She had never been on a moving chair before. Her eyes looked down and suddenly her good idea didn't seem like such a good idea. It was a long, long, long way down. Her heart beat fast. *Boom-boom, boom-boom, boom-boom.* It beat so fast she thought it was going to jump out of her body. She closed her eyes. She heard a Big Person child, on a chair going up the mountain, shout, 'Look, Papa! A marmot!'

'Geez, son. You're right!'

'And look! A rabbit!'

'Geez, son. I can't quite believe it!'

Magali crouched low in her seat, her eyes clenched shut. Her sharp claws clutched the seat, ripping into the black leather.

'Magali!'

The marmot heard Mishka calling, but she didn't want to open her eyes and she definitely didn't want to turn around.

'Magali!' Mishka shouted again. 'There! We need to jump off!'

Magali opened one eye and saw that they were a lot closer to the ground than she thought. They were coming up to a section of hilly mounds.

'Jump!' yelled Mishka.

'What?' Magali whispered. There was no way Mishka could have heard her.

'Jump now!' yelled Mishka.

Magali got enough strength to turn around and look. She saw Mishka jump off his chair and land in the hilly mounds below. He looked up to Magali and waved. 'Jump now!'

Magali closed her eyes, and let her fat body roll off of the seat. She flopped through the air. *Thump!* She landed on a green mound and rolled into a little valley. 'Ay! Ouch! Ooooh! Owwwww!' She rolled over grass, dirt, and pebbles. 'Ay yay yay!'

Mishka came running. 'Are you alright?'

'Ouch! My bottom. I landed on it.'

'Lucky it's big,' said Mishka.

Magali rubbed her bottom and felt the spot where her bald patch was. She looked around at the mounds. 'What are we doing here? Did you see something?'

'Yes. Maybe. 'Follow me.'

The rabbit hopped up the hilly mound, over the next one, and across, till he reached a crevice. It was a large grey rock that looked like it had been split into two, making a v-shape hole in the ground. They looked down into the dark space.

Mishka put his paws to his mouth and shouted. 'Andy? Dangerous?'

'Yes! Yes! We're here! Mishka!' Andy's voice called.

Mishka fell to his knees. He wiped his sweaty forehead and put his paws together. He whispered, 'Thank you, Grandpa Klaas. Thank you.'

Magali wiped her brow too and blew out a huge sigh.

Mishka shouted down into the darkness. 'Is Dangerous with you?'

'Yes, I'm here.' Dangerous Dave's voice came from below. He sounded tired.

'Don't worry! I'm here with Magali. We'll get you out!' Mishka yelled down.

Andy's worried voice came up through the crevice. 'Er, stay where you are, Man. It's really dangerous. Do you have any friends that do rescue stuff?'

Magali's eyes lit up. She jumped up and down. 'Yes! We do! We'll be back soon! Don't move!'

'Very funny,' called Andy.

'Sorry!' yelled Magali. 'We'll be back with help soon.

Promise!'

By the time Magali and Mishka found Chamois Luc, it was the afternoon. They had travelled all over the mountain looking for him. They had been to the Cheese Shack, to the hills behind the Sugar Chairlift, to the green lake, to the Bit Bumpy Piste Chairlift, to the waterfall, to the forest, and finally, they found him on the side of a mountain way up high behind the Refuge Cabin. Magali danced. She was so happy to see her friend again. The last time she saw him, he was hanging off of a cliff with a bandage on his horn.

'This is a nice surprise, My Friends,' said Chamois Luc. He looked like a goat, but bigger. He had two black stripes running up both sides of his face, covering his eyes. On his head, between his ears, two sturdy horns stood straight up. They had pointy hooks at the ends.

After climbing so high, Magali gasped for breath. 'Chamois Luc, we need your help.'

The chamois listened as the marmot and rabbit explained their tricky situation.

'And, if we don't get them back to the burrow before nightfall, my mother will kill me,' Mishka finished up the story.

'Yes,' added Magali, 'and I need to get home before

dinner. My parents have started locking the door.'

Chamois Luc nodded. His two horns moved up and down. He knelt down on the ground. 'Get on.' Magali climbed onto the Chamois's back first, then Mishka got on behind her. 'Hold on.'

They ran over the mountain, past the waterfall, past the lake, through the forest, over the Bit Bumpy Piste, over green slopes, past the Sugar chairlift, past the snakey bike trail and over to the hilly mounds to the crevice.

The rabbit, marmot, and chamois looked down into the v-shaped hole. Quite some time had passed since they'd left.

'Andy!' Mishka yelled into the darkness. Mishka waited. He looked at Magali. He looked at Chamois Luc. He frowned. He put his paws to his mouth and yelled again. 'Andy! Dangerous Dave!'

'We're here!' Dave's voice came up.

Mishka fell to his knees.

'I've got this,' said Chamois Luc, straightening up. He turned to his little friends and said, 'You two stay here. Promise me, you will not move. This is a dangerous situation and we do not want to make it worse. My Friends, do you understand?'

The marmot and rabbit nodded.

Mishka clasped his paws together and closed his eyes. 'Please Grandpa Klaas, keep Chamois Luc safe, and may he bring my cousins back safely.'

Chamois Luc bounded into the crevice. His hooves were like magnets on the rocky ground. He didn't slip, slide, skate, or fall. He simply bounded down bit by bit until Magali and Mishka couldn't see him anymore.

After five minutes, they heard Chamois Luc's hooves hitting the rocks on his way up. 'I've got them! We're coming up!'

Magali held her paw to her heart. 'Pheeeeeeeeeeew!'

Mishka wiped a tear from under his glasses.

The sun slid behind Le Grand Rocky Mountain and the afternoon slowly turned into evening. Chamois Luc trotted in the shade with four little animals on his back.

As the chamois got closer to Mishka's burrow, Andy thanked the chamois once again. 'Man, I can't thank you enough,' he said. 'We were in serious trouble there. Thank you from the bottom of my heart, yeah?'

'Me too,' said Dangerous Dave. 'We feel extremely lucky, let me tell you. Who would have thought that my cousin Mishka would be friends with a chamois? Not me, but let me tell you how grateful I am!'

'Chamois Luc is in the winter rescue service team,' said Mishka, patting Chamois Luc's back.

Chamois Luc straightened and lifted his head high.

'And that rescue team are lucky to have you, yeah!' said Andy.

Chamois Luc smiled and slowed down at the forest edge, not too far from Mishka's burrow. He knelt and the little friends tumbled off his back. 'You're welcome, Gentlemen. It's my pleasure to help a friend.'

Mishka blushed; his face changing from white to light red. His pink nose twitched too, and his whiskers shimmied. He hopped over to Chamois Luc, who bent his head. Mishka gently tugged his horn.

Chamois Luc looked at the cousins through his black stripes. 'My Friends, I hope you enjoy your visit. Can I ask? How exactly did you fall into the crevice?'

'We got chased by foxes because we wanted to see the mountain biking.'

Chamois Luc's ears flipped up straight.

Andy saw. He moved closer to the chamois. 'Know anything about mountain biking? Know any animals that might practise this sport?'

Chamois Luc's eyes lit up through his stripes. Andy

broke out in a wide smile. So did Dangerous.

Chamois Luc stuck out his chest and said, 'Gentlemen, I may well do.'

Andy and Dave high-fived each other and hopped around. 'Man, where and when?'

Chamois Luc whispered, 'Meet here tonight, as soon as the sun goes completely down over Le Grand Rocky Mountain.'

The rabbits and the marmot left the forest with massive smiles, racing towards Mishka's burrow. Magali broke off from the group saying, 'I've got to speed home. I can't be late!'

'Okay,' said Andy. 'Thanks again for your help. Let's meet tonight once the sun goes down.'

Magali shook her head. 'I'm not allowed.'

'What?' Dangerous Dave yelled. 'Just sneak out.'

Mishka stepped in and said, 'Her papa locks the door.'

'Too bad, Man!' Andy called after the marmot. 'We'll tell you about it tomorrow!'

Magali sighed and raced over the mountain. She heard Mishka's mother's voice in the distance, shout, 'There you are! We were worried sick! Where on earth have you two been?'

'Tignes.'

'Tignes? Mishka said you went to Courchevel!'

'He must have gotten confused.'

'Well, come in, we've got a nice, warm dinner for you and a clean hay bed. Bet you want to get a good night's sleep, don't you?'

A voice high up above in the treetops laughed down, 'Tcha-cha-cha-cha! Liars! Liars! Tcha-cha-cha-cha!'

Chapter 4
Kicker Cool

With her fists scrunched up, Magali paced back and forth in her bedroom. She paced so much that she made a little track in the dirt floor. At one stage, she stopped to kick her bed and bits of bark flew up in the air. She strode up and down, stomping on stray bark chips, scrunching her fists tighter. She decided to kick her bed again. *Whack!* Again, bark chips flew in the air.

All Magali could think of was Mishka and his cousins having fun at the snakey bike trails. She'd wondered if she might be able to sneak out, but she had been in the kitchen after dinner and she had seen her father lock the front door with a big bark key. Thoughts had run through her flat-shaped head. "Does he know about the time I went river rafting? Can't! I was so careful! Or, is he thinking back to my snowboarding? I told them that wasn't my fault!"

Magali had watched her papa take the key with him to his bedroom. Then, she had waited a while and when she heard *Zzzzzzz zzzzzzzzzzzzzzzzzz* she knew that her father had fallen asleep. And, when she'd heard *Ahrrrrrrr tszooooooooooooo. Ahrrrrrrr tszooooooooooooo*, she knew her mother had fallen asleep too because that was her snoring. That's when Magali had tiptoed into her parents' bedroom and started looking for the key. It was dark and she hadn't dared light the wax candle on the wall.

She reached around her parents' bark bed, the floor, and by the walls. She peered hard into the darkness, trying to see. Finally, she saw it! It was sticking out from under her father's pillow! She had reached under the pillow, and as she did, her father had rolled over, and his paw grabbed her paw. Magali froze. Her sleeping father let go and rolled over again, with his head covering the pillow right where the key was. Magali had slumped her shoulders and tiptoed back to her room.

Now, in her bedroom, she kicked her bed for a third time. *Whack!* Bark chips flew everywhere.

Andy, Dangerous, and Mishka held on as Chamois Luc trotted across the mountain slope, climbing higher up towards the Sugar Chairlift.

'Wow, you're quick, Man!' Andy shouted to Chamois Luc. 'It took us forever to climb up.'

Chamois Luc nodded his hooky-horned head.

When they arrived at the top, the little rabbits jumped off the chamois's back and looked around.

'Wow-wee!' Dangerous's mouth dropped.

'Take a look at this, Man!' said Andy, looking around. ' I knew it!'

Boar, deer, owls, foxes, rabbits, hare, hedgehogs, weasels, badgers, and chamois rode down on bikes.

Mishka's nose twitched in excitement. He pointed, 'There's even an ibex!' The ibex, like Chamois Luc, looked like a big goat too. She was sturdier than Chamois Luc. Her enormous horns curved out of her head in strong semi-circles, looping up and around like roller-coaster tracks. She rode down on her bike with a rabbit on her back, holding on to her horns with both paws.

'Yippee!' yelled the rabbit, as the ibex rode.

Chamois Luc said, 'Follow me, My Friends.' He trotted down the mountain till he reached a rocky plateau, which acted as an observation deck. 'This is a good place to watch from. Look at this badger, they say he could be the next champion.'

The badger rode down wearing a bright blue helmet. Mishka watched him ride along the snakey path. The trail rose up, and then it broke. It looked like a bridge with no bridge, just a big drop down the mountain.

The badger sped down on his bike and rode over the kicker.

'Woooooooooooaah!' Andy, Mishka, and Dangerous watched him ride over the ramp and into the air. The badger turned his handlebars left and right whilst flying and landed safely on the other side of the dirt track. He continued riding down the snakey trail.

Andy clapped his paws.

Dangerous hopped up and down.

Mishka put his paws to his mouth and yelled, 'Bravo!'

Chamois Luc looked on with bright eyes.

Next down the mountain was a deer. She came peddling down really fast, and the group watched her ride up over the kicker and into the air. She flipped her bike into a somersault mid-air.

'Totally wicked!' Andy yelled.

Dangerous and Mishka boinged up and down on the spot, clapping as they watched the deer land on the other side. Her back wheel slid in the dirt, but she stayed on her bike and kept riding.

Mishka looked up to Chamois Luc. 'This is crazy!'

The chamois nodded.

'This is nuts!' said Andy.

'This is the stuff!' said Dangerous.

Chamois Luc nodded to the next rider coming down. It was a little hare with big confidence. As he rode down, he shouted, 'Make way, Losers! I'm coming through!'

Mishka's pompom tail wiggled. 'Henri Le Hare!'

Chamois Luc nodded.

Henri Le Hare's bike flew over the kicker and into the air. Holding on to the handlebars, Henri Le Hare's body lifted away from the bike and into the air, like Superman.

'Wow!' gasped Dangerous.

The little hare landed on the other side of the trail, holding his paw in the air. He shouted, 'And that's how it's done!' He disappeared down the trail.

Chamois Luc nudged Mishka to look up the mountain.

Mishka looked up and gasped. 'F-F-Foxy!'

The chamois nodded.

F-F-Foxy rode his bike up and over the kicker, into the air. He spread his legs out before bringing them back to the pedals. He landed on the other side and shouted to the hare in front, 'I'm better than you!'

Chamois Luc nudged Mishka again. Mishka looked up. Another fox came riding down.

Little Foxy's bike flew off the kicker and he frontflipped into the air, somersaulted, then landed on the other side, with his back wheel landing on the very edge of the ramp. He wobbled.

'Uh-oh!' said Andy.

Dangerous started shaking his head.

Their eyes fixed on Little Foxy's back wheel. Their eyes darted from the wheel to the large gap, then back to the wheel. The tyre bounced off the edge, and Little Foxy used his weight to bounce the bike forward. He continued to hop along on his bike. He hopped three or four times before managing to bring his front wheel down, then he rode down, following his brother and the hare.

Mishka blew out a sigh of relief. 'Phew!'

'This is wicked!' Andy said, beaming up at the chamois. 'Thank you for bringing us, Man!'

Suddenly, a puppy Saint Bernard, wearing a red helmet with a sticker on the front saying *I didn't do it,* came racing down the mountain. He flew over the kicker, flipped his handlebars in a barspin and landed on the other side.

Dangerous shook his head in disbelief. He looked up to the chamois. 'We've got to do this. Any chance you know how we can have a go?'

The chamois smiled and said, 'As a matter of fact, Gentlemen, Mishka and I know some guys who might be able to help.'

An hour later, much further down the mountain, Henri Le Hare hopped up and down in front of Chamois Luc, Mishka, and the cousins.

Chamois Luc had brought the rabbits through the forest, running alongside the bike trail. They had followed it till they ran out of the forest and into a big circular clearing. This was the end of the trail. This is where the animals gathered to check their bikes and take a rest before riding back up the mountain.

Mishka heard a deer say to her ibex friend, 'Are you alright?'

The ibex stood by her mountain bike. 'Yeah. Thank goodness I bailed before I hit that tree!'

'I know! I saw. I nearly had to, too. I went too fast on the last corner.'

Next to them, two owls were congratulating each other. They flapped their wings together.

'That trail was dope!' said the first owl.

'Totally!' said the second owl.

To the right, a fox and a badger high-fived each other, whilst still on their bikes. Mishka heard the fox say, 'Man, that was nirvana!'

The badger laughed and said, 'You said it, Bro. Did you see me? I went so much faster when I hit that downside.'

'Yeah, I saw you! Man, that last kicker is wicked. So dark in the forest though.'

'I know! It's tricky. I nearly spun out a few times.'

The fox lifted his paw for another high five and the badger slapped it.

The cousin rabbits looked around at the animals. They looked at how close they were to foxes and owls. Mishka patted his cousins' shoulders. He had explained previously about the No Eating Other Animals At Night sports rule.

Henri Le Hare shook his head. 'Sorry, Dudes, no

can help. It's nearly impossible to get a bike around here. No-one has a spare one.'

'There is that one dude,' said F-F-Foxy, stepping forward. 'He rents out bikes.'

'Who?'

'The boar with the black, f-f-fuzzy ears,' said F-F-Foxy.

'Dude, he's bad news. Forget it,' Henri Le Hare said.

F-F-Foxy shrugged. 'I don't know. I heard he had bikes.

'Where is he?' Andy asked.

'I said, he's bad news.'

'Up by the top of the Sugar chairlift, to the left,' said F-F-Foxy.

'We'll try!' said Dangerous, his eyes beaming at Andy.

Henri Le Hare shrugged his shoulders. 'Don't say I didn't warn you! S-later, Dudes! Meet us tomorrow night at the top of the Sugar run.' He rode off on his bike.

'See you tomorrow,' F-F-Foxy smiled, following the hare.

Little Foxy saluted as he rode away, following his

brother and the hare. Puppy Bébé bubbled, 'See you tomorrow!' The puppy had a voice that sounded like he was speaking through bubbles. It sounded like he said, "Blub blub blubblorrow!"

Andy rubbed his paws together. He looked at the others. 'Boar? Tomorrow night?'

Dangerous looked up at the moon. 'Yes, we don't have time tonight. It's bedtime.'

Mishka raised his eyebrows.

Chamois Luc scraped the ground with his hoof. 'Gentlemen, maybe you should take Henri Le Hare's advice.'

Andy waved the chamois's advice away. 'Nah! We need bikes, Man. It will be fine!'

Dangerous hung his arm around his brother's shoulder. 'Yeah! What's the worst that can happen?'

A voice very high up in the trees laughed down. 'Tcha-cha-cha-cha! Tcha-cha-cha-cha!'

Chapter 5
Plan B

The next night, Dangerous, Andy, and Mishka knelt by Magali's burrow under the moonlight. Andy pushed the little wooden door. Nothing.

Dangerous got behind Andy, and they pushed together against the door. Their long bunny ears flopped over their noses as they tried to force the door open. Nothing.

Then Mishka got behind Dangerous, and the three of them pushed. Nothing.

Andy said, 'Plan B.'

The three rabbits walked one metre to the left of the front door and started digging.

'She better be there,' whispered Dangerous.

'She will be,' whispered Mishka.

'Hey, don't dig so roughly,' said Andy. 'We've got to fill it back up tonight when we bring her back, remember.'

Magali stood in the darkness in her kitchen. She smiled and jumped up and down when she heard the digging noise. She was going to be able to go mountain biking! Mishka had told her all about it this afternoon.

'They were flying over a kicker, then there was a big gap, and if they didn't time it right, they would fall way way way down, but if they got it right, they landed on the other side of the track. It was crazy! Some of them were doing somersaults mid-air! And Frontflips! Lots of tricks! And, when they landed on the other side, they just kept riding down the trail, easy as. It was nuts, okay! Like nuts, nuts, nuts, yeah?!'

Magali's eyes had glistened as she listened to every word falling out of Mishka's mouth.

The rabbit had continued. 'And then, you won't believe who we saw coming riding down, yeah?'

'Who?'

'Henri Le Hare, F-F-Foxy, Little Foxy, and Puppy Bébé!'

'What?!'

'Yeah!'

'I want to go!'

'Didn't you find the key?'

'Yes, but he sleeps with it under his pillow. I tried to grab it, but he grabbed my arm. I thought I was going to pass out.'

'So, there's no way you can sneak out?'

'Not that I can think of.'

The rabbit had scratched his long ear and said, 'Hmmmm, there must be a way.'

Magali silently jumped up and down in her kitchen in the dark. She looked up to the wall. The scratching was getting closer. They had told her they were going to make a hole just big enough for her to squeeze through. After a few minutes, she felt bits of dirt tumbling down and soon she saw a sliver of the moon peeking through! She put her paw in her mouth, trying to hold in a happy squeal. More and more moonlight streaming in. When she could see clearly, she stuck her arms through the hole.

'There she is!' Andy said. 'Pull her out.'

Dangerous grabbed Magali's arms and started lifting

her out. Her head popped out. 'Evening!' Dangerous whispered.

Magali giggled.

Dangerous kept pulling, but Magali got stuck. The top half of her body was sticking out of the burrow, but the fat bottom half was stuck inside.

'We told you not to eat too much at dinner!' whispered Dangerous.

'I didn't!'

'Suck your stomach in.'

Magali took a deep breath in, and Dangerous pulled with all his force. She shot out of the burrow like a champagne cork. *Pop!*

Under the moonlight, the three rabbits and marmot held their paws over their mouths, trying to hold the laughter in. They high-fived each other.

'Quickly,' whispered Andy. 'We need to cover the hole.'

They covered the hole with bits of grass, leaves, and bark that they had found earlier.

'Let's go. Chamois Luc is waiting!'

Magali's heart felt like a happy tornado was going through it. She took some deep breaths as she followed the others to their meeting point.

Later, when they reached the top of the Sugar Chairlift, Chamois Luc knelt down so his little friends could climb on. He raced to the left and looked around. 'He should be somewhere near here,' he said. 'Look for black, fuzzy ears.'

Snort! Snort!

The chamois turned around. Behind him stood a stocky boar. He was definitely the ugliest boar Magali had ever seen. His body was round like a wine barrel. He had short, brown, bristly fur. He looked half-shaven because half of his bristly fur was missing down his back. His snout was super long, too long for a normal boar. Magali stared at the circular base of his snout where his wet nostrils were, then her eyes travelled back up the long snout to his eyes. They were really small. This boar didn't look quite right. Magali looked at his ears. His eyes may have been small, but his ears definitely weren't. They were enormous, and black and really fuzzy. It looked like all the lost fur from his back had somehow made its way to his ears. Magali blinked, looking at the unfortunate-looking boar.

'Did someone say fuzzy ears?' said the boar.

The friends jumped down from Chamois Luc's back.

Andy hopped close to the boar. 'Man, we heard you had some bikes.'

The boar stood back, looking at the rabbits, the chamois, and the marmot. He looked to Andy and said, 'That's an interesting accent you have.'

'I'm Dutch.' Andy smiled.

'Welcome to France.'

'Thanks, Man.'

The boar lifted his snout up high and said, 'I have some bikes to rent. How many do you need?'

'Four,' said Andy.

Chamois Luc had said earlier that he had his own bike stashed away.

'Follow me,' said the fuzzy-eared boar. He trotted over a hilly mound and behind another hilly mound, and behind yet another hilly mound, till he stood at an old wooden shack. The boar pushed the loose wooden door open.

Andy, Dangerous, Chamois Luc, Mishka, and Magali stepped inside.

Andy's smile grew wide when he saw the little bikes.

The boar motioned for them to select a bike to try. Magali grabbed a red bike. It had pink and white streamers coming out of the handlebars.

Andy chose a blue and black bike with fat tyres. 'Excellent, Man. How much to rent for one night?'

They had heard earlier in the day that the price was five apricots per bike. After dinner Mishka, Andy, and Dangerous had offered to do the washing up. Then, whilst they were in the kitchen, they had snuck into the cupboard and stolen 20 apricots.

'20 apricots,' said the boar, his miniscule eyes twinkling.

'Great,' said Andy, getting ready to pass over the fruit.

'Per bike,' said the boar.

'What?'

'Twenty apricots per bike. There are four of you. Twenty times four equals 80 apricots.'

'That's too much!' said Dangerous.

The boar shrugged.

Andy, Dave, Mishka, and Magali stood looking at their bikes.

Mishka sighed.

So did Magali.

Andy lay 20 apricots on the ground for the boar. 'We have 20 apricots. That's five apricots each. That's the fair price. Take it or leave it.'

The boar shook his head. 'Sorry. No can do.'

Andy looked at Dangerous, Mishka, and Magali as he got on his bike. There was a twinkle in his eye. 'Sorry. We can't either.' He shot the others a look and he started pedalling. 'Come on! Let's go!' He pedalled out of the shack and away over the mountain.

Dangerous was a second behind him. 'Hurry!' he shouted to Mishka and Magali.

Chamois Luc had already started racing away.

Mishka and Magali froze, looked at each other, then jumped on their bikes, and rode after Andy and Dangerous.

The boar shouted after them. 'Stop! Stop!'

Andy shouted back to the boar, 'We'll bring them back at the end of the night, Man!' He rode up a mound and down a mound, laughing into the night air.

Dangerous and the others rode after him. 'Yoo-hoo-hoo!'

Chamois Luc raced alongside. 'Gentlemen, this was perhaps not a good idea.'

Mishka and Magali's little legs pedalled as fast as they could to keep up.

They rode up the last mound near the Sugar Chairlift. At the top of the mound, they saw them; a line of fat boar waiting on the other side. The heavies were scraping their hooves in the dirt and snorting into the night air.

'Uh oh,' said Andy, looking at the mean boar.

'This was not a good idea,' said Dangerous, looking at the boar's thick bodies and strong hooves.

The boar lowered their heads. Hot air blew out of their large nostrils.

'They're going to charge!' shouted Chamois Luc, kneeling on the ground.

'Abort! Abort the mission!' yelled Andy, jumping off of his bike and running onto Chamois Luc's back.

The heavy boar, with their long snouts pointing down, charged up the mound. Their hooves dug into the ground, sending dust flying up in the night air.

'Eeeeeeeeeeeeeeeeeeeeeee!' Magali jumped off her bike and onto Chamois Luc's back.

Mishka and Dangerous did the same.

The eight boar charged, using the full weight of

their bodies to pummel forward. Chamois Luc got up and ran. He bounced over the mountain, and the rabbits and the marmot held on for dear life. The chamois kept running till they were way past the Sugar Chairlift and down by the kicker observation place.

Chamois Luc blew out a heavy sigh and took some deep breaths as knelt down to let the group off.

'Oh my goodness!' said Magali. Her fur was standing up straight in shock.

Mishka's ears were sticking up as straight as a board.

Dangerous's eyes were red. 'I don't know that that was a good idea, Man.'

Andy paced up and down. 'It was a good idea! He's a thief! 80 apricots! That's ridiculous! He's a thief! He heard my accent and thought, "oh, here comes some easy apricots." That's not fair! I left our apricots. I gave him the right price!' He paced up and down, his pompom tail wiggling.

Dangerous put his paw on his brother's shoulder. 'Yeah, he's a thief. Yeah, he wanted to rip us off. But maybe running away with the bikes was not such a good idea.'

'Yes, it was!'

Dangerous looked over to Mishka and Magali, then

back to his brother. 'Not if we have others to think about, hmmmmm?'

Andy said, 'How are we going to get bikes now?'

Chamois Luc stepped forward. 'Gentlemen, and… ' he nodded to Magali, ' …Mademoiselle, I'm sorry it didn't work out. But, I have to go for my own bike. I keep it hidden behind one of the rocks much higher up. I want to get some runs in tonight. Let's meet here later in the night, okay?'

'Thanks, Man,' said Andy. 'Sorry for putting you in that situation.' He looked at the others. 'That goes for all of you.'

Mishka stuck his chest out. 'We'll find another way!'

Magali straightened up, too. 'Yeah!'

Dangerous nodded. 'Yeah! We will not be beaten!'

Chamois Luc laughed. 'That's the spirit! I'll see you later, My Friends!' He bounded up the mountain, under the moonlight.

The group turned to watch the animals coming down on their bikes. Once again, the animals rode up over the kicker, into the air, and landed on the other side.

Magali jumped up and down, squealing with delight. 'Eeeeeeeeeeeeeeeeeeeeeeeeee!'

The others jumped up and down too, cheering the riders on.

'Way to go!'

'Gnarly!'

'Awesome!'

'Wicked!'

A badger came riding down to the kicker with a very serious look on his face.

Andy said, 'He's coming down too fast. Man, is he going to make it?'

The badger flew over the kicker, into the air and landed on the other side, his back wheel skidding in the dirt. The group watched as the badger fought to hold on to his bike, riding with one wheel on the ground, the other in the air. He managed to get control back and brought the two wheels down onto the track. He kept riding the snakey trail.

'Phew!' said Andy.

Next to come down the trail was a young Saint Bernard dog.

Magali gasped. 'Puppy Bébé!'

Mishka smiled.

Wearing his red helmet, Puppy Bébé came riding down the trail. He rode up the kicker and barked as he flew into the air. *Ruff! Ruff!* He did a Tailwhip and landed.

Magali jumped up and down. Her eyes shone even more brightly when she saw Henri Le Hare, F-F-Foxy, and Little Foxy ride down one after the other. She laughed and cheered as each one rode over the kicker.

'Wicked!' shouted Magali at the top of her voice.

Mishka laughed as he watched her reaction.

'You know those guys, too?' Andy asked Magali.

The excited marmot nodded.

Dangerous pointed up the mountain. 'Look! He's coming.'

Two hooked horns came riding down the mountain. The group looked on with eager eyes as Chamois Luc rode down, towards the first kicker. He flew over it and into the air. They whooped and cheered.

'Woooooo-hoooooo!'

'Go for it, Man!'

'Yes! Yes! Yes!'

'Go, Chamois Luc!'

The group shouted, laughed, and clapped as they watched their rescuer friend fly through the air, do a 360, then land on the other side.

Laughing, Andy shook his head. 'Oh Man, that looks like so much fun! We've got to find a way to get some bikes. But how?'

Mishka looked up to the moon and the stars, took a deep breath and said, 'I think I might have an idea.'

Chapter 6
Recycling

'Here she comes!' Mishka's tail jiggled and wiggled. 'Magali!' he waved, 'we're here!'

Magali raced down the mountain and into the forest edge.

'Hello,' she greeted the rabbits with a kiss on either cheek.

'Did they see it?' Dangerous asked.

'No!' Magali smiled.

Dangerous high-fived Magali, so did Andy and Mishka.

Last night, after they'd watched a lot of mountain biking tricks, Dangerous had looked up to the moon and said, "Time for bed." Andy had nodded in agreement. Mishka and Magali had looked at each other and shared shoulders shrugs. Dangerous had led the group back over the mountain to Magali's burrow, and they had pushed Magali back through the freshly dug hole, saying, 'We're going to fill in the hole from this side. You need to pat it down and make it look smooth from your side. Use some water to keep it in shape. Make it nice and smooth. And remember to sweep the floor. Make sure no dirt is lying around. Okay?'

This morning, Magali had woken up earlier than everyone else just to double-check the kitchen wall looked okay. She had used some water last night to make the dirt stick properly. This morning she had looked at it closely and smiled at her handy work. No obvious traces! She had scurried back to her warm bark bed with a fat smile on her face.

At the bottom of the mountain, Andy peeked through the trees, over towards the start of the Sugar chairlift. Big People were moving forward in the queue, ready to get on with their bikes. 'Mishka. What is your idea for our bikes?'

'Better be better than Andy's,' laughed Dangerous.

'Follow me,' said Mishka, hopping further into the forest.

Magali smiled. She liked discovering new places. They ran down through the trees until they came out of the forest edge, where there was a road. They waited till there were no cars, then they raced over the gravel road and disappeared into the little forest on the other side.

'Tcha-cha-cha-cha!' laughed a voice from high up. 'You're up to no good! No good! Tcha-cha-cha-cha!'

Magali gasped, looking up to the treetops. 'Who are you?' she shouted.

The rabbits looked up, too.

'Tcha-cha-cha-cha!' Up to no good! Tcha-cha-cha-cha!'

'Ignore him,' whispered Andy. 'Let's keep moving. Where are we going, Mishka?'

Mishka led them through the trees, to the edge of the little forest. They looked out to a village dotted with wooden chalets. They crouched low, careful to stay in the trees. Then, they followed Mishka past the village and around a bend, all the while staying inside the edge of the forest. They travelled along until finally, down below, they saw a grassy clearing in the distance. In the middle of the clearing was a big steel building standing.

'This is it,' said Mishka, crouching.

'What is it?' asked Magali, looking at the large building. The tall, sliding front door was open. Inside, lots of Big People stuff was piled up on top of each other: old tables, chairs, sofas, beds, cables, mattresses, microwaves, ovens, fridges, planks of wood, skis. Wait a minute. Magali looked closer. Skis?! And snowboards?! Tossed around, lying on top of each other? When she saw what lay next to the snowboards, Magali gasped. 'Bikes!'

'I don't believe it!' whispered Andy.

'Me neither!' said Dangerous. He patted his cousin on the shoulder. 'You're a genius, Mishka. This is a great idea!'

'Yes!' Magali jumped up and down, clapping her paws.

'How are we going to get them?' whispered Andy.

'Don't know.'

They looked down. A Big Person was walking out of the spacious building and starting to slide the tall door closed.

'Oh no! He's going to lock it up!'

'We need to get in there now!'

'Look!'

A different Big Person pulled up in his red truck. 'Hello, Mike! Can I quickly dump some stuff?' he said, jumping out of his truck.

Big Person Mike looked at his watch. 'Okay, but pull the door closed behind you when you leave. It's lunchtime, and I promised my wife I wouldn't be late.'

'Will do. Thanks.'

The group watched as Big Person Mike left in his car. The second Big Person unloaded a bed frame, a cupboard, and a yellow kid's bike from the back of his truck.

'I can't believe it!' Mishka hopped up and down as he looked at that bike.

'That's a sign!' whispered Dangerous.

As soon as the Big Person drove away, the group scuttled down to the door. The Big Person had closed it, but there was a little gap. Mishka sucked his stomach in and squashed through. The others squashed in after him. They had to help Magali cause her plump bottom got a bit stuck, but they managed to pull her in. Inside, they high-fived each other. Then, they went scrambling to find a bike each. Mishka found the yellow bike immediately. Andy found a white one. Dangerous found an orange one. Magali turned around and around, looking.

'Here, this one!' Andy pointed.

Magali shook her head. 'Too big.'

'This one!' whispered Dangerous.

'It's missing its pedals.'

'So? We'll make some!'

'No,' whispered Magali. She turned her head left and right. Her eyes searched. All the bikes were too big. She breathed in and out, trying to hold back tears.

Suddenly, they heard the noise of a car pulling up.

'We've got to get out! Hurry!'

'They're going to see us!'

Mishka pointed. 'Back door! Look! Hurry!'

Magali saw a bright green scooter with a broken handlebar on top of a pile of wooden planks. She picked it up and followed the boys out the back door. When they reached the forest, the others stopped to look at Magali and her scooter.

'What's that?'

Magali smiled. 'It's better than nothing!'

The rabbits burst out laughing. 'Ha ha ha!'

Andy high-fived Magali. 'Good thinking, Magali! Ha

ha! That's clever!'

'Tcha-cha-cha-cha!' laughed a voice from high up. 'You're up for lunch! Tcha-cha-cha-cha!'

The group froze. Their fur rose up, their ears stuck up, and their whiskers froze.

A low growl came through the trees.

Grrrrrrrrrrrrrrrrrrrrrrrrrrrrrrrrrrrrrrrrrrrrrrrrrrr.

'Ride!' Andy yelled.

They jumped on the bikes and scooter, then raced through the tall trees.

Grrrrrrrrrrrrrrrrrrrrrrrrrrrrrrrrrrrrrrrrrrrrrrrrrrr.

Magali looked back and saw large yellow eyes following her. She gasped and pushed harder on her scooter, turning right. She rode out of the forest trees and towards the village.

'What are you doing?' yelled Andy.

'She's right!' yelled Mishka, sensing the growling animals getting closer. 'We're safer in the village. Come on!'

The rabbits rode over rocks and dirt till they reached the village.

Magali scooted across the road and behind a large

chalet. She hid in the back garden under the apple trees. The rabbits joined her.

They heard a Big Person child say, 'Marmot! Rabbit! Rabbit! Rabbit!'

Then they heard another Big Person say, 'Did you see a rabbit and a marmot, Ethan? Wow, what a lucky boy you are! Now, come inside and wash your hands. It's time for your sleep.'

The group hid by the apple trees, looking across the road to the forest on the other side.

Yellow eyes paced up and down in the darkness of the forest edge. They would not come into the village.

Magali put her paw on her heart and blew out a big sigh. 'Pheeeeeeew!'

'Tcha-cha-cha-cha!' laughed a voice from high up. 'Nearly Dead! Nearly Dead! Tcha-cha-cha-cha!'

Magali shook her paw up at the tree-voice, too scared to shout anything. She looked at her rabbit friends. Sweat trickled from their foreheads and their chests rose up and down as they tried to get their breathing under control.

Magali looked down to her beautiful broken-handle scooter. A big smile broke out on her face. She whispered, 'Dudes, tonight we ride!'

Chapter 7
Locked Horns

'Hey! Hey! Hey! You found bikes!' Henri Le Hare smiled when he saw them arrive. 'And you think you're going to start here? On this Black Trail? Do you want to break your bones? You need to start on the Blue Trail, Dudes!'

'Evening!' Two foxes slinked past them and as they smiled, their sharp fangs poked out.

'Evening,' Henri Le Hare replied with a friendly wave.

Andy, Dangerous, Mishka, and Magali stared at the foxes. Sweat started to run down Magali's forehead as the image of the fox's nose pushing his way into the burrow hole flashed in her mind. Mishka, Andy, and Dangerous sweated, too.

F-F-Foxy slapped Magali's shoulder. She jumped with fright. 'Relax,' said F-F-Foxy. 'Remember the rule? No Eating Other Animals At Night. Not while we do sports.'

Little Foxy bulged his eyes as he looked at the bald patch of skin on Magali's fat bottom. 'But, not in the daytime!' His tongue rolled out of his mouth.

F-F-Foxy smacked his brother on his head. *Bof!* Little Foxy kicked his brother in the knee. *Whack!* F-F-Foxy growled and jumped on Little Foxy, forcing him to the ground. They rolled and bit each other. F-F-Foxy gave a warning growl as he rolled his brother over and over until eventually, he shoved his face down in the dirt. *Grrrrrrrr.* Little Foxy wriggled under his brother, his tail wagging.

'Time out!' called Henri Le Hare. 'Focus, please.'

The brother foxes jumped up, shaking out their bodies. Shake shake shake. Bits of red fox fur flew in the air.

F-F-Foxy moved forward and said, 'Blue might be too easy. They could start with the Red Trail.'

Chamois Luc stamped his hoof in the ground. 'They need to start with Blue.'

Little Foxy looked at Magali and Mishka. 'Yes. Definitely Blue.'

Puppy Bébé looked up at the moon in the sky and started counting stars. 'One, two, three, four... '

Henri Le Hare looked at the beginner bikers. 'You start with Blue. If it's too easy, you move to the Red. Follow me.' He got on his bike and cycled down to where the mountain became less steep. He stopped in front of a snakey bike trail. He pointed, 'This is the Blue.' Then, he pointed diagonally across the mountain in the other direction. 'Over there is the Red. Got it?'

The three rabbits and the marmot nodded. Henri Le Hare smiled and tapped Magali and Mishka's heads. They were wearing their snowboarding helmets. Mishka's long ears stuck out of two holes in his helmet.

Henri Le Hare, F-F-Foxy, and his friends were wearing their helmets with two holes too. Chamois Luc didn't wear a helmet.

He had said, "Ears *and* horns. I'm not doing it."

Henri Le Hare clapped his paws. 'Okay. We'll do one Blue with you to get you started. Ooops, we'll just let these guys pass first.' He moved back to let two ibex pass.

'Evening!' called the first ibex as he rode past. He was enormous, with two impressive, solid, semi-circle horns coming out of his head. They were so large that they looked like they were too heavy for his head.

The second ibex rode past next. He was enormous too, and like the first ibex, he had a thin, pointy beard under his chin. 'Evening!' he called.

'Evening!' they replied.

Henri Le Hare looked at his group. 'Come on!' He pushed off down the Blue Trail. Magali followed. Next was F-F-Foxy, followed by Mishka. Then there was Chamois Luc, then the cousins, then Little Foxy, and finally Puppy Bébé. They travelled down the snakey path.

Magali smiled, feeling the loose dirt under her scooter as she rode over flat parts, then up and over small bumps. 'Eeeeeeeeeeeeeeeeeeeeee!' she squealed up to the moon.

'Remember to stay loose on your bike!' Henri Le Hare yelled. 'Don't try to control it, you'll waste energy. Just let it go and you direct it.'

F-F-Foxy yelled, 'And don't brake suddenly! You'll end up f-f-flipping your bike!'

Little Foxy called from the back of the line, 'Shift your weight from side to side!'

'Gentlemen, and Mademoiselle, you'll get a feel for it, the more you do it!'

Puppy Bébé looked up at the night sky. 'Eight, nine, ten, eleven...' He cycled along, one eye on the stars, one eye on the trail.

'Woo-hoo!' Andy called out. 'This is grand!' It was certainly a lot different to cycling in flat Holland.

'Excellent!' called Dangerous Dave, peddling on his newly stolen bicycle.

'Peddle faster! There's a climb coming up!' Henri Le Hare peddled fast, building speed. He raced down into a dip. Then he rode up the climb using the momentum from the dip. As he got to the top of the climb, he stood up on his bike and peddled hard to finish the climb.

The others followed behind, doing the same. Magali had to push her scooter along with one foot on the ground, pushing and pushing.

Henri Le Hare waited for them at the top.

They arrived with huge smiles spread across their faces.

'Woo! That was pretty easy!' Dangerous smiled.

'Yeah, I reckon we could try the Red Trail,' said Andy.

Mishka and Magali nodded.

Little Foxy looked over Henri Le Hare's shoulder and frowned. He pointed in the distance. 'Do you think we should step in?'

The two ibex who had passed them earlier were off their bikes and fighting each other on a flat clearing by the track.

'I won!' shouted the first ibex.

'No, I did!' shouted the second ibex.

They lowered their horns, ran towards each other and smashed horns. *Crash!* The sound of solid horns crashing against each other rang out through the night air. Slowly, little animals came out of the trees to see what was going on. A rabbit, a couple of hedgehogs, a badger, and a fox circled the ibex, watching them fight. The ibex charged again, and their horns smacked against each other once more. *Crash!*

'Ooooooh!' Little Foxy sucked in his breath. 'This is not good.'

Henri Le Hare hopped over, past the spectating animals, and over to the ibex. 'Hey! Hey! Hey! Cut it out! You're scaring the hedgehogs!' He pointed down to two hedgehogs who were not scared at all. 'Stop!'

The first ibex lowered his head, ready to charge.

The spectating animals put their paws over their mouths. 'Ooooooooooooooooooooooooh!'

The second ibex lowered his head. They charged and their horns crashed together. *Crash!*

'Ooooooooooooooooooooooh!' the animals gasped.

The hedgehogs' spikes spiked up. 'Fight! Fight! Fight!' they shouted.

The ibex's heads were lowered and their horns were still pressed together. In fact, they had locked horns. The first ibex tried to pull back, but he took the second one with him. The ibex moved back and forward, shaking their heads, trying to free themselves.

'That's enough!' called Henri Le Hare. 'Break it up, now.'

'Uhm, we can't' said the first ibex, pushing the second one.

The second one pushed back. 'Ugh! We're stuck!'

'What do you mean you're stuck?' asked Henri Le Hare.

The spectating animals watched as the heavy ibex pushed back and forth, trying to free themselves. But their horns were truly stuck together.

'Ugh!' grunted the first ibex. 'Could you give us a hand? Could you get us unstuck?'

Henri Le Hare's eyes grew wide. 'Oh, now you want *us* to help *you*? A minute ago, when we asked nicely for you to stop fighting, you wouldn't. But now, suddenly, you need our help? Is that what I'm hearing?'

'Come on, Man!' begged the second ibex, with his head lowered, facing the ground.

'Hmmmm, we'll we're going to have to think about it,' said Henri Le Hare, looking back to his group of friends.

The hedgehogs started giggling.

'Ugh! Don't leave us like this. Please!' called the first ibex. 'My neck is starting to hurt.'

'Mine too,' said the second ibex. His thin, pointy beard blew back and forth.

F-F-Foxy and Little Foxy moved forward.

'Come on, Man. Let's put them out of their misery.'

'We're not magicians!' said Henri Le Hare, but he moved forward with the foxes, and they grabbed hold of their horns. 'One, two, three... Pull!' Henri Le Hare pulled one way. The foxes pulled the other.

The spectating animals looked on, clapping and cheering.

'Yeah! Pull harder!'

'Set them free!'

'Come on! Pull!'

The foxes and hare pulled with all their might, but the ibex were still stuck together.

A spectating badger and fox jumped up. 'We'll help.' They joined Henri Le Hare's side, and the animals pulled again.

The hedgehogs cheered them on.

'You can do it! Pull harder!'

They tried as hard as they could, but the ibex were really stuck together.

Finally, Chamois Luc trotted over.

'Gentlemen, stand aside,' he said. The little animals made way, and Chamois Luc took a few steps back to get a run-up. He lowered his head and charged straight towards the ibex's locked horns. His sturdy, hooked horns bumped into the ibex's horns with just enough force to shift them. The ibex quickly separated and lifted their heads up high.

The spectating animals jumped up and down.

'Hoorah!'

'You did it!'

'Well done!'

'Life-saver!'

Tilting his head from side to side and stretching his neck, the first ibex trotted to Chamois Luc and said, 'Thanks, Mate.'

The second ibex blushed. 'Yeah, thanks, Dude.'

They got on their bikes and rode away.

Henri Le Hare waved and called after them. 'No goodbye? You leave just like that?'

F-F-Foxy laughed. 'They were embarrassed.'

'I would be too,' said Henri Le Hare. He looked at the spectating animals. 'Show's over, Dudes. Get out of here!'

The little spectators trudged off back to the forest.

Henri Le Hare looked at F-F-Foxy, Little Foxy, Puppy Bébé, and Chamois Luc. 'Are we ready?'

Little Foxy's eyes lit up. 'Let's do it!'

Puppy Bébé's tail wagged.

'We've only got tonight left to practise!' said F-F-Foxy, chasing his tail. 'I've got to perfect my Backflip!'

'I've got to practise my Barspin.' Little Foxy jumped up and down.

Puppy Bébé's dopey eyes shone. 'I'm going to see if I can do the Can-Can.'

'I'm going to do a Frontflip.' Chamois Luc's eyes shone through his black stripes.

Henri Le Hare boinged up and down on the spot, his little tail flopping around. 'We need to be extra, extra, extra prepared!'

'Prepared for what?' asked Magali, feeling like she wanted to jump up and down too.

'For what?! For what?!' said Henri Le Hare. 'Only the best competition ever!'

'Yes!' said Chamois Luc. 'The Tricky Tricks Competition. It's tomorrow night!'

'You know that fox from Courchevel?' Little Foxy said.

'The one who won last year?'

'Yeah. Well, he's coming back tomorrow night.'

F-F-Foxy stuck his chest out. 'Well, he better be ready to lose, cause I'm going to win with my f-f-famous 360!'

'No, I'm going to win!' Henri Le Hare held his paws

in the air.

'I am!' Little Foxy chased his tail.

'I am!' barked Chamois Luc.

Puppy Bébé wagged his tail and looked up to the moon.

Aaaaouuuuuuuuuuuuuuuuuu!

The foxes howled too.

Aaaaouuuuuuuuuuuuuuuuuuu!

All the dogs in the mountain howled.

Aaaaouuuuuuuuuuuuuuuuuuuu!

'What do you have to do in the competition?' Magali asked.

'Your best tricks,' said Henri Le Hare, before stopping to look squarely at Magali. 'Why? You want to be in it, Squealer?!'

Magali shrugged her shoulders.

Getting on his bike and riding away, Henri Le Hare laughed. 'Nah! See you tomorrow night in the Bike Park! You as a spectator!'

Chamois Luc and Puppy Bébé followed him.

F-F-Foxy got on his bike too. He looked at Magali

before riding away. 'Tomorrow night, we'll show you how it's done!'

Little Foxy followed his brother. As he rode away, he laughed and said, 'Magali win the competition? She doesn't even have a bike, Mate! She's got a Scooter! Ha ha ha! Nooooooooooooooooooooo way!'

As Magali watched her friends ride away, a little fire burned in her heart.

'Tcha-cha-cha-cha!' laughed the tree-voice from high above. 'Don't even think about it! Tcha-cha-cha-cha!'

Chapter 8
Red Trail

'Did you see him? He nearly hit the tree!'

'Yeah, I saw him, Man. He missed it by a centimetre!'

'Totally gnarly.'

Magali listened to Andy and Dangerous Dave talking about a deer they had seen on their first red run.

After the ibex fight, they had ridden back up the mountain and found the Red Trail. Andy had gone first, then Mishka, then Magali. Dangerous Dave had been at the back. They had gone down the curly trail, riding slowly over the dirt, enjoying the sensation of rolling in and out of the path. The first time they came across a kicker, Andy had called out, 'Kicker coming up! Keep your front wheel up!' He had flown over the small ramp and landed back down on his back wheel.

Mishka had closed his eyes and held on tight to his handlebars as he rode over the kicker. He landed perfectly.

Magali had ridden up and squealed as she went into the air. 'Eeeeeeeeeeeeeeeeeeeeeeeeee!' She grasped the handlebars tightly. Then, she felt the bump of the scooter as it landed back on the dirt path. She let out a huge sigh. 'Pheeeew!'

Dangerous Dave followed her. He had gone over the little kicker and landed well, too.

'Wow! That was so cool!' yelled Mishka as he followed Andy down the bike path.

'I know!'

'I love it!'

'Yoo-hoo!'

The little group continued along the snakey path till they got to the next fun trick. It was a long stretch of dirt that went up and down like a gigantic caterpillar. They smiled as they rode up and down, and up and down, and up and down, all along the mountain trail. After a while, they got to another kicker ramp. This time, it was bigger. Andy called out, 'Kicker coming up!' He flew over the kicker, holding tightly to his bike bars. As he flew through the air, he took his feet off the pedals and spread his legs out wide. 'Woohoo!' He landed back on the path with a smile.

Mishka was next over the kicker, but he was less confident. He didn't try to stick his legs out or anything, he just kept his eyes straight ahead. He landed back on the dirt with a big bump and a wobble, but managed to stay upright on his bike.

Magali was next. She instinctively bent down low on her scooter as she flew over the kicker. She landed safely on the other side.

Dangerous Dave went over the kicker last. He turned his handlebars left and right in mid-air. 'Yeah!' he shouted into the night air.

The group's eyes lit up under the moonlight as they followed the Red Trail down towards the forest. The moon disappeared as they rode into the forest and through the trees. Everything became dark, and they rode more slowly. They continued towards the next trick: a kicker with a big gap before the next ramp. It was like riding over an open drawbridge.

As Andy rode along in the darkness, he noticed something out of the corner of his eye. On the ground, riding alongside, he saw two little beady eyes belonging to a long viper. The snake was travelling beside him. Andy pedalled faster. The snake sped up. Andy slowed down. The snake slowed down.

'We've got company!' Andy shouted back to the others.

'I know!' shouted Mishka. He had looked down to his right and had seen a snake travelling alongside him too.

Magali and Dangerous Dave had viper snakes on the ground next to them too.

Andy was so distracted with his snake that he didn't pay enough attention to the path. When his bike went over the kicker, he hadn't had enough speed. His bike went into the air, and instead of landing over on the other side, he fell in the gap. He plummeted and crashed on the dirt ground below. *Smack!*

Mishka did the same thing. He landed beside his cousin. *Smack!*

Next to fall down the gap was Magali. *Crash!*

Dangerous managed to fly over the kicker with enough speed that he landed, with a slight bump on his back wheel, on the other side. He braked in the dirt, looking down the gap.

'Are you alright?' called Dangerous.

Andy shifted, stretching out his body, checking for broken bones.

Mishka blinked and readjusted his helmet and glasses.

Magali got up, brushing dirt from her fur. She picked up her scooter. 'I'm alright!' she shouted.

'Me too!'

'Me too!'

Dangerous Dave waited at the top. He looked around, trying to see if the snakes were still on the other side of the kicker. He peered across in the darkness. Nothing. Then, he looked down to his feet and all around him. Nothing. Only dirt and trees.

When the others reached him, he said, "What was that all about? The snakes?!'

'Don't know.'

'Mine was looking at me like, all mean-like, like he couldn't wait to kill me.'

'Mine didn't look mean.'

'Mine looked weird. Kind of like he liked sliding alongside me.'

'Same with mine. It was very strange.'

'Mooooooove!' A deer came riding down the mountain path towards the kicker.

Andy and the others quickly shuffled off the dirt trail. They watched the deer fly over the kicker with good speed. She flew into the air, turned her handlebars from side to before landing, right before their eyes, on the dirt path, and continuing down.

'Bravo!' shouted Mishka.

'Wicked!' shouted Magali.

Next, a badger on a bike that was missing one pedal, came riding down.

'Wooooooaaaaah!' the badger cried as he flew into the air, flipping his bike into a 360-degree spin. He landed perfectly, in front of the group, and kept riding.

'Cool, Dude!' Andy congratulated the badger.

'Well done!' shouted Dangerous.

The rabbits and the marmot stayed there watching animal after animal ride over the kicker, then land before them on the other side. There was a fox, followed by a chamois, then a badger, then a boar, then finally an eagle.

Magali sucked in her stomach when she saw the eagle. Sweat trickled down her back.

Mishka put his paw on Magali's shoulder. 'Remember, it's nighttime.'

The little marmot breathed out heavily.

The Eagle gripped on to his bike and flew into the air. His wings spanned out and carried him and his bike over the gap. He landed before them on the path.

The group clapped and cheered.

'Thanks, Dudes,' the eagle called, before disappearing down the dirt track.

Andy whispered, 'That's cheating a little bit, if you ask me.'

'Still impressive,' said Dangerous.

'We need to speed up like they did,' said Andy. 'Did you see how they pedalled faster before getting to the kicker?'

They all nodded.

'Also, lean into the bike more,' Dangerous added.

'Let's finish this trail, then get back to the top to do it again!' Andy smiled, getting on his bike. He looked up to the moon. 'We've got time for one more ride, then it's bedtime.'

Magali and Mishka looked at each other and shared a questioning shrug.

They got on their bikes, looking back uphill to check no animals were flying down before rejoining the bike trail. They pedalled through the trees.

Sssssssssssssssssssssssssssssssssssssssssssssssssss.

'I don't believe it!' said Andy, looking down and pedalling faster.

The four of them pedalled as fast as they dared to on the curvy bike path, but as fast as they pedalled, the snakes were still there, moving beside them, leaving thin snake tracks in the dirt.

Sweat poured down Magali's face as she looked down to her weird-looking snake.

Sssssssssssssssssssssssssssssssssssssssssssssssssss.

Andy shouted down to his snake. 'What do you want? Huh? What?'

'Tcha-cha-cha-cha!' laughed a voice high up in the treetops. 'Viper fangs! You're dead! Tcha-cha-cha-cha!'

Magali looked up. 'Don't say that!' she yelled as she rode over a bump.

'Tcha-cha-cha-cha! Snake bite! Snake bite! Tcha-cha-cha-cha!'

'Stop it!' yelled Magali to the treetops.

'Tcha-cha-cha-cha!'

Sssssssssssssssssssssssssssssssssssssssssssssssssssss.

The snakes broke off to the right. They slid away from the path and disappeared into the heart of the forest.

At the same time, Andy followed the path out of the forest, arriving into a plain, wide mountain clearing, with the moon shining down. He veered his bike around and pulled up to a stop.

The others pulled up next to him.

'Look!' pointed Andy, looking further down the mountain to another big clearing. 'The Bike Park! That must be where the competition is tomorrow night!'

They rode closer and watched a team of boar, badgers, weasels, and chamois working to build a dirt, semi-circle ramp. On the other side, more animals were building a small kicker, a medium kicker, and a very high kicker.

'Jeez Louise!' said Dangerous, pointing to the highest kicker. 'Who is going to ride over that? It's crazy!'

Magali's black eyes lit up watching the busy team in the bike park. Her heart raced. 'Maybe we should enter?'

'What?' they looked at her.

'Maybe we should enter the competition tomorrow night?'

'Are you mad? Have you seen the others?'

'You only have to do tricks.'

'So?'

'So... we've got the rest of the night to practise!' The young marmot's eyes beamed. 'We might win!'

'Tcha-cha-cha-cha!' laughed the voice from above. 'You might die! Tcha-cha-cha-cha!'

Chapter 9
Tricky Tricks Night

'Suck your stomach in,' whispered Dangerous, lifting Magali out of the hole. He dragged her up and onto the ground. They placed the leafy cover carefully over the hole, then raced across the mountain under the moonlight.

Mishka ran next to Magali. 'Are you sure they don't know?'

'Nothing!' Magali smiled, racing over rocks and grass.

They sped to their hiding place by the mounds behind the Cheese Shack. They got their bikes, then rode down towards the Bike Park.

'Don't go so fast!' Magali called, but the boys were already way ahead. They were running a little late because Magali hadn't been there straight away when they'd shown up. She had had to wait a little because tonight her father had decided he wanted to have a second helping of his blueberry dessert. Then he wanted to have a cup of piping hot, bark tea. As her Papa was drinking his tea, Magali stood by the door, praying her father, mother, aunt, and uncle wouldn't notice the circle in the wall. The colour of the dirt was a little bit different, where the hole was. Magali shifted from foot to foot, watching her father drink the last gulp of tea. Her aunt looked over to Magali's moving feet.

'What's that?' she said, bending down to look at the loose dirt at Magali's feet.

Magali's eyes nearly popped out as she saw her aunt bend to touch the loose dirt. Her knee jerked up and hit her aunt in the face. *Bam!*

'Oh! Ouch!' her aunt screamed, jerking back with the pain. 'Ouch! My nose!'

Magali's uncle came running over. 'Princess, what happened?'

Magali's mother came running, too. She put her arm around her sister's shoulders, whilst looking back to Magali and saying, 'Have you lost your mind, Magali?'

'I can't see!' Magali's aunt cried, holding her nose.

Magali looked at her aunt's face. The left eye was really red. 'I'm so sorry! It was an accident!'

Magali's mother ushered her sister and brother-in-law away from the kitchen. 'Come to the bathroom. We'll put some water on your face. 'As she led them out of the kitchen, Magali's mother looked back to her daughter with a stern look.

'Sorry!' Magali called after her aunt. 'It was an accident!' She took a deep breath in and looked over at her father.

He'd finally finished the last swallow of tea and, without saying anything, decided it was time for bed.

Soon after, under the moonlight, Magali scooted over the bumpy mountain ground. 'Wait for me!'

Further down the mountain, she could hear competition sounds in the still of the night; sounds of animals singing, laughing, and chanting. She rode downhill on her scooter till she caught up with Mishka and his cousins at the Bike Park. It was the same large circular area they'd seen yesterday. Tonight, it was full of adrenalin-charged animals of all sizes, on bikes. The full moon hung low in the sky. Perfect conditions for a competition.

'Look at all these dudes!' said Andy. He scratched the curly fur on his head as he looked at the crowd.

Boar, weasels, hare, chamois, foxes, rabbits, owls, eagles, badgers, ibex, and deer were doing last-minute checks on the air in their tyres.

Magali looked around. Next to the semi-circle ramp, there was the bumpy dirt path with kickers of three different sizes. Animals were already riding up and over them, warming up. Henri Le Hare, F-F-Foxy, Little Foxy, Chamois Luc, and Puppy Bébé stood near the largest kicker. 'There they are!' Magali pointed. 'Come on! Let's join them!'

'Hey! Squealer! You made it!' Henri Le Hare greeted Magali with two kisses. *Mmmwua. Mmmwua.*

Little Foxy said, 'Still going to enter the competition?' He pointed to a fox flying mid-air on his bike doing a 360-degree spin. 'Cause you need to be better than that guy.'

Magali looked down at her scooter and back to the flying fox. She straightened her shoulders and said, 'Yes! I'm going to try. Everyone's allowed to start somewhere.'

'Me too!' said Mishka.

Andy said, 'We're going home tomorrow. We've got nothing to lose, right?!'

Dangerous nodded. 'There are so many animals here tonight. Surely not all of them are experts?'

Chamois Luc stomped his hoof in the ground. 'Magali is right. Everyone needs to start somewhere!'

'Wow-wee, there's a pig!' Mishka pointed to a fat

little pig riding down the path and over a kicker. He landed on the other side without falling from his bike.

F-F-Foxy pointed left to a group of deer. 'They've come over f-f-from Tignes.'

Little Foxy nodded towards a group of boar. 'They're from Val D'Isere. And, see that group of foxes? They're from La Rosiere, definitely not from around here.'

Puppy Bébé bubbled, 'Those owls over there are from Meribel. They're supposed to be good.'

Chamois Luc pointed his horns to a group of chamois. 'Those chamois are from Val Thorens. I've heard about them, but I don't know them.'

Henri Le Hare moonwalked up and down. 'Doesn't matter, Dudes. Cause I'm homegrown. I'm from La Plagne and I'm going to win!' He smiled and fastened the strap on his helmet. His hare ears stuck up super straight out of the two holes.

F-F-Foxy's triangular ears stuck up straight out of the little holes in his helmet, too. 'I don't think so. I'm going to win!'

An ibex's voice came over the loudspeaker. 'Ladies and Gents, welcome to La Plagne's Tricky Tricks Bike Night!'

The animals exploded, cheering and shouting.

'Hoorah!'

'Yee-haa!'

'We're going to shred it tonight!'

'We're going to fly!'

'Extreme riding, Dooooooood!'

Magali jumped up and down, clapping her paws.

The ibex's voice came back over the speaker. 'We've got a bit of everything for you tonight! And a bit of everyone. We've got guys all the way from Chamonix!'

A group of badgers strutted into the centre of the park, holding their striped black and white heads up high.

The ibex's voice continued. She said, 'And we've got guys all the way from Val D'Isere!'

The boar trotted into the middle of the bike path, lifting their snouts in the air. They chanted, *We're here to win! We're here to win! We're here to win!*

Henri Le Hare put his paws to his mouth and sang, *'You're here to lose! You're here to lose! You're here to lose!'*

The ibex's voice continued. 'My name is Mountain Melody. I am your host for tonight. Once again, welcome to this fantastic Bike Park, right here in beautiful La Plagne!'

Henri Le Hare bounced up and down. 'Right on!'

Chamois Luc shouted, 'You said it!'

Magali and Mishka linked arms and danced around and around.

Puppy Bébé and the brother foxes let out an almighty howl up to the moon.

Aaaaaoooooouuuuuuuuuuuuuuuuu oo-oo-oo-ooooo.

Each animal in the park clapped, cheered, and laughed.

The ibex continued, 'This is a one-night competition where each rider has one chance, and one chance only, to show us his or her best bike tricks. The rules are to respect safety, respect each other, and keep it clean. We have the medical team here. Please give a huge round of applause for Medical Ed The Eagle and his flying doctor team!'

Four eagles swooped down from tree branches and zoomed into the centre of the Bike Park. They criss-crossed each other, flying back and forth, and in out, like fighter jets in battle. *Zip! Zoom! Zip! Zoom!*

Magali's heart raced. She always remembered her mother's words. "If you see an eagle, get in the burrow. You don't want to end up like your poor cousin. He tried to run, but the eagle swooped down and picked him up with its cruel claws. It carried your cousin away, back to its nest and eagle babies. I don't want to think about what happened to him." Magali took a deep breath and remembered the night sports rule. Plus, all the other animals around her were going nuts with applause. They yelled up to the eagles.

'Wow! The Flying Doctors!'

'You guys rock!'

'We love you!'

'You're the best!'

'Look at them go!'

'Power Gods!'

'The best!'

The powerful eagles hovered in circles, dipping low, and in and out of the cheering animals.

The ibex's voice came back, laughing. 'Thank you Medical Ed The Eagle and your team!'

The fast eagles did one last tour of the Bike Park before flying back to their observation positions high up in the tree branches.

Mountain Melody's voice came back. 'Competitors, we wish you the very best of luck! Last year's winner was from Courchevel... '

The Courchevel foxes trotted into the circle, carrying the champion fox on their backs. The confident fox lifted his paws in the air.

The spectating animals cheered and whooped.

'And this year, who knows!' shouted the ibex's voice. She continued, 'These are the guidelines: You go over the kickers one by one. First, there is the small kicker. If you make it over that, you get to the next kicker which is a bit bigger. If you make it over that, you get to the final, freaky, funky kick-kick-kickerrrrr!'

The animals went crazy again, erupting into cheers and whoops.

Puppy Bébé and the brother foxes howled with extra energy.

Aaaaaooooouuuuuuuuuuuuuuuuuu oo-oo-oo-ooooo!

Henri Le Hare jumped up and down, shouting, 'La Plagne! This year's winner is from La Plagne! You're looking at him!' His skinny body boinged up and down, and his tail wiggled a million miles an hour.

The ibex's voice said, 'Dudes and Dudettes, we invite you to take your place in the line, and we wish you the best of luck! Let's get started!'

Animals shuffled forward, fastening their helmets and checking their bikes one last time.

Henri Le Hare and F-F-Foxy pushed each other as they tried to get in front of each other in the line.

The ibex's voice shouted, 'First, we have... looks like a pig! Wow! I think it's the first time we've had a piglet in the competition. Come on young man, off you go. Show us what you can do!'

The piglet pushed off.

The animals cheered him on as he rode down the long dirt path towards the first kicker. Everyone stayed silent as he rode up and over the kicker.

The ibex's voice commentated. 'Oooooh, nice lead-up to the kicker and he's in the air. Good twist of the handlebars, and he's landed back on the path! Now he's coming up for the second kicker, it's a lot steeper, he needs a lot more speed. Watch him! Watch him! Watch him... he's over the kicker and in the air! Again a nice twist and turn of the handlebars and... Ooooooooooooooh!'

The piglet missed the landing. He fell and slid down the gap, crashing at the bottom. *Crash !*

The spectators shouted out.

'Are you alright, Man?'

'Are you hurt?'

'Tough luck, Dude!'

'Help's on the way!'

A medical eagle flew in, swooped down, stretched out his razor-sharp claws and picked up the piglet. He carried him away to Sickbay.

Mountain Melody continued. 'Next up, it looks like we have a young deer from Tignes! She looks ready to go! When you're ready, Mademoiselle.'

The deer pushed off.

Like the pig, she did a good jump over the first kicker but lost it at the second. Two medical eagles flew in, picked her up and carried her to Sickbay.

'Oh, look who's next!' Mountain Melody called. 'It's last year's winner, the fox from Courchevel! Best of luck to you!'

The confident fox rode down over the first kicker and into the air, spreading out his legs in the air as he flew.

Mountain Melody, the ibex, kept up the commentary. 'He's lifted his body up! He's doing the Superman! And, he's landed well. Ha ha ha! A couple of nice Bunny Hops now but will he get enough speed for the second kicker? Yes! He's done it, with a very nice handlebar spin too. What about the third and final, freaky, funky kicker?'

The spectating animals watched on. Their whooping

and cheering died down as they watched the fox's legs pedal fast.

The fox rode up high over the final kicker.

'He's in the air! He's doing a Frontflip 360! Bravo!'

The fox spun his bike around in the air and landed on the other side of the dirt path, skidding a little. He punched his strong paw in the air.

The spectators went nuts.

'Woo! Woo! Woo! Woooooo!'

'Champion!'

'Gnarly, Man!'

'You're the Man!'

'Wicked!'

'Rad!'

'Magic!'

'Courchevel! Courchevel! Courchevel!'

Henri Le Hare and his group moved forward in the queue. The night progressed, with most of the competitors falling down at the second kicker. The medical eagles were constantly flying in to lift them up and take them to Sickbay.

'Excuse me?' a white spotty deer with big brown eyes tapped Andy's shoulder.

Andy smiled. 'Yes?'

'I'm part of the organising committee.' She pointed to Andy and Dave. 'You two can't participate without a helmet, sorry. You need to move out of the queue.'

'What?!' Andy looked around.

'Where are we going to find a helmet now?' Dangerous looked around, searching the ground for a spare helmet.

Mishka said, 'You can wait till Magali and I go through, and then you can use our helmets.'

'No,' said Andy, shaking his head. 'There won't be enough time. Look how fast the line is moving.'

'Sickbay!' Dangerous Dave smiled. 'We'll go to Sickbay and ask those dudes!'

They moved out of the line, riding towards Sickbay.

'Hurry up!' Mishka called after them. He took a step forward in the line. His tail wiggled with excitement when he saw how close it was to his turn.

Mountain Melody's voice came through the loudspeaker. 'Next, we have another deer from Tignes! Off you go!'

The deer rode down and over the first kicker.

'Oh no she didn't!' called Mountain Melody. Her voice went super high in pitch. 'She did a 360 mid-air as her very first trick! Her first trick! And now she's shredding down the path, getting ready for the second kicker. Will she make it? Yes! She's in the air and, oh my goodness, she's gone into a Frontflip on an axis! This girl is on fire! And she landed well. Now she's going for the final, freaky, funky kicker. Will she do it? She's in the air, and... she's gone into a backflip! Look at her go! Oh! Oh! Oh no! She missed the landing! She's down! She's down. Is she hurt? Uh-oh. Four eagles have flown in. Is this serious? Oh yes, I can see. It's a broken bone. Oh, what a shame! Such talent! I'm sure that's not the last we've seen of her. Come back next year! Okay, who's next? We've got an owl from Les Menuires.'

The owl crashed into the mud wall of the second kicker. He was lifted to Sickbay with a broken wing.

After the owl, it was a boar. He lost it after the first kicker and got lifted to Sickbay with a fractured hoof.

Next was a badger from Les Arcs. He fell short of the landing on the second kicker. An eagle took him away with a fractured shoulder.

'Oh my goodness!' called Mountain Melody, the ibex, through her loudspeaker. 'Ladies and Gents, it is carnage tonight. Sickbay is overloaded with hurt animals. Mountain Biking is an extreme sport indeed. So far, we've only seen the fox from Courchevel make it through the entire course. Will we see anyone else make it through? I can't believe I'm saying it, but maybe we won't!'

Henri Le Hare yelled out, 'Dude! Please! You hurt my feelings!'

F-F-Foxy yelled out. 'Yeah! You haven't seen anything yet!'

Chapter 10
Extreme Downhill

'Who do we have next?' Mountain Melody called the next competitor forward.

F-F-Foxy shouted, 'Me!' but the hare took off like a rocket. *Ziiiiiip!* Off he rode towards the first kicker.

The spectators whooped and cheered. 'Go, go, go!'

The ibex called the race. 'Okay, so we have a local guy from La Plagne. This hare is riding up to the first kicker and oooooooh, he's in the air, he does a very nice Barspin. Now he's on to the next kicker. Will he make it over the second kicker? Yes! He's in the air doing a 360! Man! Look at how he yanks that bike around! Wow, that was nice! He's making it look so easy! He's back down on the path, going for the final, freaky, funky kicker. Will he be the second competitor to make it all the way through? He's off into the air! Wow! He does the Truck Driver; and... he lands! HE'S DONE IT! HE'S DONE IT! HE's MADE IT ALL THE WAY THROUGH!'

Henri Le Hare punched his scrawny arm up in the air and shouted, 'Wooooooo-hooooooooooooo!'

The spectating animals cheered.

'Way to go, Brother!'

'Yes! Yes! Yes!'

'Totally!'

'You did it, Man!'

'Too cool for school!'

'You're the man!'

'Awesome!'

F-F-Foxy's tail wagged at super speed as he got on his bike. His determined eyes fixed straight ahead.

The ibex's voice came over the speaker. 'Next, it's another local. Let's see what this fox can do!'

F-F-Foxy pedalled the path.

Magali watched him crouch low on his bike as he got close to the first kicker.

F-F-Foxy flew over into the air, stretching out his arms and legs like superman flying through the air.

Magali shouted, 'Woo-hoo!'

F-F-Foxy landed on the other side, then started pedalling towards the next kicker.

'Go F-F-Foxy!' Magali cheered. Her almond-shaped eyes were as wide as they could open as she watched F-F-Foxy fly over the second kicker.

Mountain Melody called it. 'He's doing a reverse flip! What a trick! Did you see that? Wow! And will this guy make it to the end of the course, too? Certainly looks like it!'

All eyes were fixed on F-F-Foxy as he rode up to and over the final, freaky, funky kicker. He took off into the sky.

'AN OFF-AXIS 360! HE'S LANDED! HE'S LANDED!' The ibex's voice shouted through the loudspeaker. 'He's done it! What an incredible run! Wow, it's going to be hard to call a winner! Ladies and Gentlemen, we have three competitors through now!'

Magali and Mishka bounced up and down. Mishka's glasses nearly fell off.

'Next, another local! This group are all locals. This chamois is from La Plagne. He should know the territory. Will he make it all the way through? Hang on a minute, this guy is not wearing a helmet!'

Chamois Luc flew over the first kicker and did a Barspin. On the second kicker he did a Hop Whip, and on the third kicker he did a Frontflip! He landed as smooth as can be, then looked up to see all the animals screaming and cheering his name.

'Chamois Luc! Chamois Luc! Chamois Luc!'

The excited ibex's voice spoke really fast through the loudspeaker. 'Oh boy! The local boys are really showing us how it's done tonight! Wait a minute... Oh no, I've just heard the chamois from La Plagne will be disqualified because he isn't wearing a helmet! Shame! He did some fabulous tricks! Okay, who's next?'

Mishka's nose twitched a hundred miles an hour. His whiskers flickered. His heart raced.

Magali squealed as her friend pushed off on his stolen bike. 'Eeeeeeeeeeeeeeeeeeeeeeeeeeee! Go, Mishka!'

The ibex watched Mishka pedal. 'This next contestant has a sense of humour. Check it out! We have a rabbit doing the Bunny Hop down towards the first kicker. Don't know if he's going to have enough speed for the kicker. Ooooooh, he's over the kicker, and... no! Not enough speed! He's down on the ground! An eagle has flown in. He's picking him up. There he goes. Off to Sickbay. Who's next?'

Aaaaaaaaaaaaaaauuuuuuuuuuuuuuuooooooooooooo.

Puppy Bébé howled to the moon as he rode down to the first kicker.

Magali didn't know whether to whoop for Puppy Bébé, or be worried about Mishka.

Ssssssssssssssssssssssssssssssssssssssssssssssssss.

Four snakes appeared at Magali's feet. She frowned.

Ssssssssssssssssssssssssssssssssssssssssssssssss.

Little Foxy, standing in front of Magali, hissed down at the snakes. 'Sssssssssssssssssssssssss yourselves! Get out of here! You think you're going to be in the competition? Ha ha ha! Get out of here, I said!' His foot struck at the snakes, just missing them. He looked back up to cheer on Puppy Bébé, who had just made it over the third kicker with his Can-Can trick.

'HE'S DONE IT!' Mountain Melody called. 'He's the fourth to have made it through to the end. This competition is getting tough. We only have two more competitors to go. Come forward next competitor!'

Little Foxy's eyes shone as he jumped on his bike, but then he frowned. He looked down at his wheels.

Sssssssssssssssssssssssssssssssssssssssssssssssssss.

The viper snakes disappeared in the grass.

Little Foxy's face was a second away from exploding.

'Next competitor, come forward please!' the ibex called.

Little Foxy burst out in an angry howl.

Aaaaaaaaaaaauuuuuuuuuuuuuuuuuuooooooooooooo!!

Magali looked down at Little Foxy's bike tyres. Two viper-sized puncture marks sat in both flat tyres. Magali saw Little Foxy's face turn bright red, redder than his fox fur.

The ibex called, 'Next competitor! Come forward!'

Magali pushed her scooter forward. 'Here, take this.' She slumped her shoulders as she offered her scooter, but when she saw the light in Little Foxy's eyes, she knew she had done the right thing.

'Thanks, Magali!' Little Foxy whipped the scooter from her paws and raced off down the path.

The watching boar, deer, weasels, foxes, hedgehogs, badgers, hare, owls, chamois, and rabbits pointed and laughed at Little Foxy.

The ibex's voice laughed too. 'Okay, well it is on wheels, so it fits in with the competition rules. Let's see what this fox can do. He's over that first kicker and boy oh boy is he flying through the air! I don't believe it. He's done a 360 right off the first kicker!

Wow wee! He's landed and going for the second kicker! Seems like a determined type of guy. He's off over the kicker into the air, and... wow! He's done a double reverse flip! I can't believe it! Here he goes over the final, freaky, funky kicker, and... HE'S DONE A 360! Oh my goodness and A SECOND ONE! 720!' The ibex's voice was at full volume. 'HE'S DONE A 720! Wow! Wow! Wow! This is incredible! What an amazing evening here in La Plagne, and what a way to end the show, Ladies and Gentlemen! My heart is pumping so very fast!'

The animals who had laughed at Little Foxy at the start were now whooping and cheering at full volume. Some of them were bowing down to him. They chanted, 'Champion! Champion! Champion!'

The ibex's voice came loud and clear over the speaker. 'You saw it with your own eyes. A double Frontflip! We have a new Champion and it's a little fox from La Plagne on a green scooter!'

The animals ran to Little Foxy, surrounded him, and lifted him up on their shoulders.

Magali smiled as she looked over to Little Foxy receiving the adulation. She didn't join the cheering crowd, she decided to head down to Sickbay.

Andy and Dangerous carried a hedgehog through Sickbay, to the back room.

Magali saw Mishka's cousins. 'You two! What happened?'

Andy said, 'It was so busy when we got here. They needed our help.'

A girl rabbit hopped past, stopping to pat Dangerous on the arm. 'Thank you so much! We don't know what we would have done without your help!' Then she patted Andy's arm. 'Both of you. Thank you.'

Blushing, Andy and Dangerous carried the hedgehog to the waiting nurse in the back room.

'Mishka!' Magali saw her friend and raced to him. 'Are you okay?'

Mishka sat, wearing his helmet. 'I'm fine,' he said. 'I feel totally fine, but they wouldn't let me go back out. They said they had to double-check I didn't have concus-something.'

Magali held up her paw. 'How many paws am I holding up?'

'One.'

'You're fine. Let's go. We have to get back. Little Foxy just won!'

'What?!'

'On my scooter!'

'What?!'

'Did you just say Little Foxy won the competition?'
Andy came hopping over.

Dangerous came hopping too. 'On your scooter?'

'Yes!' Magali laughed. 'We have to go and join them.
It's a big party!'

Andy and Dangerous Dave walked over to the
rabbit nurses. 'Veronique, Dorothee, it was cool
hanging out with you tonight, but we have to go. If
you're ever in Holland, be sure to look us up!'

The two nurse rabbits giggled and waved goodbye.

Back at the competition area, over-excited deer,
foxes, boar, weasels and badgers surrounded Little
Foxy.

Magali found Henri Le Hare and the others just
next to them.

'Not fair!' Henri Le Hare scrunched up his paws.

'He didn't use a bike!' F-F-Foxy's face was tomato-
red.

'I should have won!' Henri Le Hare pouted, sticking
out his bottom lip.

'No. *I* should have won!' said F-F-Foxy, sticking out his chest.

'I was better than you!'

'No. I was better than you!'

'I did better tricks.'

'No. I did!'

'You want to make a bet?'

'Yeah!'

Henri Le Hare picked up his bike.

F-F-Foxy picked up his bike.

'You're on!'

'Let's go!'

The two animals pushed off down the mountain.

Puppy Bébé jumped on his bike. He bubbled to the others, 'Come on! We'll follow them!'

Chamois Luc rode after the puppy.

Mishka ran to his bike and called to Magali. 'Jump on!'

'What?'

'Hurry!'

Magali jumped on the back of Mishka's bike. They looked back to Andy and Dave, but Dave pointed up to the moon, put his head against his paws and closed his eyes.

'Seriously?' called Mishka. He shrugged his shoulders and shouted, 'Okay! See you back home later!' Mishka pushed off down the mountain, following the others. They bumped up and down over rocky mountain ground and headed straight towards the Big People's village below.

'There they are!' Magali pointed. Chamois Luc and Puppy Bébé had stopped at the top of a hill.

'Look!' said Chamois Luc when they caught up. He nodded down to the village twinkling with chalet lights. 'Look at what they're doing.'

Magali's eyes widened as she saw Henri Le Hare and F-F-Foxy in the distance, riding over a bridge. Not on the bridge, but on the rails of the bridge. Then, they rode over a stretch of mountain and jumped from the mountain onto the flat roof of a big building!

'Oooooooh!' Chamois Luc, Puppy Bébé, Magali, and Mishka watched with wide eyes.

The hare and the fox rode over the roof and when they got to the edge, they flew off the edge, and landed on the rooftop of a chairlift station!

'Ooooooh!' the friends cried again.

Henri Le Hare and F-F-Foxy manoeuvred their bikes from the top of the chairlift, onto the ground, bouncing down, and landing perfectly.

'Ooooooh!' the group shook their heads in disbelief.

The hare and fox took off and rode into the village, towards a steel grid staircase.

'Wicked,' bubbled Puppy Bébé.

Henri Le Hare and F-F-Foxy rode down the long metal staircase, turning left on the flat part in the middle, then right, down the rest of the metal staircase. F-F-Foxy's fangs banged together as he rode down the stairs. *Clac-clac-clac-clac-clac-clac.*

'Ooooooh!' the group cried, watching. They kicked off on their bikes to follow the hare and the fox.

The hare and fox rode along till they reached the edge of the mountain, then they flew over the side!

'Come on!' Chamois Luc said.

They scrambled on their bikes to follow again and got to another point in the mountain where they had a good view. They pointed down to Henri Le Hare and F-F-Foxy. They had landed on to another roof top.

'Crazy!' bubbled Puppy Bébé.

'This is nuts!' said Chamois Luc, his eyes fixed on the racing duo.

Magali and Mishka watched on, shaking their heads in disbelief.

Henri Le Hare and F-F-Foxy raced over the sloping roof, off the edge, and landed on garbage cans. *Clang, clang, clang!* A family of slimy worms came out and shouted, 'What do you think you're doing!' The hare and fox continued over the garbage cans, then headed for a bridge.

The friends scrambled on their bikes to follow. Puppy Bébé and Chamois Luc shredded down the steep slope, pedalling hard.

Mishka tried to keep up, but he skidded on the dirt. His front tyre locked. The yellow bike flipped. He and Magali went flying.

'Wooooooooaaaaaaaaaaaaaaahhhhh!' Mishka flapped his arms up and down in the air.

'Wooooooooaaaaaaaaaaaaaaahhhhh!' Magali cried, her legs cycling mid-air.

They landed in a great big heap on the hard

mountain ground. *Thump! Thump!*

'Ouuuuuch!' Magali rolled over. 'Ooooooh! Ouch, wowch, ouch!'

'Owwwww ay ya yay!' Mishka's eyes had turned red. His nose twitched. He rolled over and turned to Magali. 'Are you okay?'

'Am I okay? We just flew through the air, Mishka!' she said, rubbing her bottom. 'I landed on my bottom. It really hurts.'

Grrrrrrrrrrrrrrrrrrrrrrrrrrrrrrrrrrrrrrrrrrrrrrrrrrr.

Magali and Mishka froze. They heard the noise again, in the still of the night.

Grrrrrrrrrrrrrrrrrrrrrrrrrrrrrrrrrrrrrrrrrrrrrrrrrrr.

'Foxes!' whispered Mishka, his eyes bright with fear.

A different, more dangerous growl came from the right.

Gggggggggggggggghhhhhhhrrrrrrrrrrrrrrrrrrrrrrrr.

'Wolves?' gasped Magali, tears springing into her eyes. She shivered in fright and a patch of her fur fell out of her bottom. She reached to feel the bald patch of skin. It was the size of three cherries. She started to cry.

Mishka huddled closer to Magali. 'We're going to get

eaten alive.'

Magali whispered, 'Say a prayer to your Grandpa. Quick!' Her heart beat extra fast. *Boom-boom, boom-boom, boom-boom.*

Grrrrrrrrrrrrrrrrrrrrrrrrrrrrrrrrrrrrrrrrrrrrrrrrrrr.

Gggggggggggggggghhhhhhrrrrrrrrrrrrrrrrrrrrrrrr.

Whoooooooooooooooooiiiiiit!

Four medical eagles hovered above. In their sharp claws, they held a corner of a forest mat made of bark, twigs, and twine. The eagles stretched the mat out, flying low to the ground.

Medical Ed The Eagle shouted, 'Get on!'

The marmot and rabbit leaped onto the mat just in time. The eagles to lift them into the air. They flew straight up in the sky, away from the growling animals.

Mishka bent his head. 'Thank you, Grandpa Klaas.'

Magali didn't dare look over the side of the mat. She didn't want to see which animals nearly got them. Wiping her tears, she lay back on the mat. She looked up to the eagles' powerful wings, stretching above her in the night sky. The medical team flew higher and higher in the air. Magali lay back and closed her eyes. She wished for the eagles to take her straight up and leave her on a star. She wished to live on a star for one year. A little voice popped into her head. The voice was the moon, and it said, "Magali, you don't want to live on a star. It will be lonely on a star. Didn't you have fun with your friends? Didn't you have fun on the dirt trail and the kickers? You don't need to live on a star, Magali. You just need to learn how to have fun, without danger. Be smarter."

Magali sat up and opened her eyes. She breathed in the fresh pine smell from the treetops. She took one deep breath after another. She sat still on her forest mat until she felt her heart beating at a normal speed.

She leaned over the side of the mat, looking down in the trees. She searched and searched, but she couldn't see him. She scratched her head. She shouted to Medical Ed The Eagle. 'How did you know we needed help? How did you know where we were?'

Medical Ed The Eagle nodded up ahead to more treetops coming up. 'We got a tip-off.'

When they flew over those treetops, Magali looked down. She saw him. On the top branch sat a fat, fluffy owl with a large white circle on the top of his head. He laughed up and waved. 'Tcha-cha-cha-cha! Tcha-cha-cha-cha!'

Magali laughed at the cheeky owl. 'You! Thank you! You're really annoying, but thank you! '

Next to him sat his brother with fat, black eyebrows.

He laughed up at Magali. 'Brrrrrrrrrrrrrrrrrrr ruppp ruup rupp!'

Next to that fat, black eyebrows owl sat another owl with eyes as big as the moon. 'Hee hee hee. Ha ha ha!'

Wiping a tear from her eye, Magali blew kisses to the cheeky owls. 'Thank you! You saved us! Thank you very, very, very much!

The Eagles flew higher up into the night sky, away from the young laughing owls. Magali smiled wearily and breathed out a very long sigh. 'Pheeeeeeeeeew!'

Rubbing the bald patch on her bottom, she reflected on her mountain biking adventure. She thought back to the fun and wonderful stuff; her green scooter, the moving chairlift, the Blue Trail, the Red Trail, the ibex's horns stuck together, the weird snakes, and the freaky, funky, final kicker. She laughed into the night air and waved. 'Goodbye Mountain Biking! Later, Dudes!'

THE END

Dear Dude

I hope you liked the book AND the illustrations. Guess what? I drew the illustrations myself. and you can too! Drawing is so much fun. I used the internet for help with a lot of the drawings. I typed in "How to Draw a/ an (plus the name of the thing I wanted to draw)". It's really cool to have artists sharing their tips on how to draw. Check out these helpful sites:

Articco Drawing, Draw so Cute, Genevieve's Design Studio, 365 Sketches, Drawing Tutorials 101, Calvin Innes, Easy Pictures To Draw, Art For Kids Club, 5 Drawing Art, HT Draw, Drawing Tutorials 101, Harriet Muller, Color Drawing Book, PiKasso Draw, How To Draw, KidArtX, Limo Sketch, How To..., Channel, GuuhMult, Art For Kids Hub, Yo Kidz, We Draw Animals, DrawStuffRealEasy, DrawIn Geek, Azz Easy Drawing, Cam Plapp, howtodrawa, how2drawanimals, Katrina Doodles, Happy Drawings.

We've reached the end. If you fancy leaving a review, that would be super cool (authors lurve reviews!). You could say something short and sweet about something you liked (with the help of an adult). Cheers big ears!

Tcha-cha-cha-cha! Tcha-cha-cha-cha!

Best wishes
Muddy

Facebook and website: Muddy Frank Books

French Marmot Dude Series (English version)

Dude's Gotta Snowboard
Dude's Gotta River Raft
Dude's Gotta Mountain Bike
Dude's Gotta Paraglide
Dude's Gotta Bobsleigh
Dude's Gotta Rock Climb
Dude's Gotta Paintball
Dude's Gotta Wakeboard

Magali Marmotte Série (French version)

Help ! Suis Accro Au Snow
Help ! Suis Accro Au Raft
Help ! Suis Accro Au VTT
Help ! Suis Accro Au Parapente
Help ! Suis Accro Au Bobsleigh
Help ! Suis Accro À L'Escalade
Help ! Suis Accro Au Paintball
Help ! Suis Accro Au Wakeboard

And Bilingual Version / Et Version Bilingue (English Français) Magali Marmotte Série

Check out the colouring books in the same series for kids 4-8 years! Magali Marmot's Mountain Bike Adventure.

Made in the USA
Las Vegas, NV
24 August 2023